RECKLESS SEDUCTION

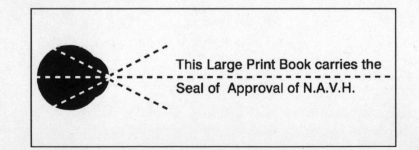

This Large Print Book carries the
Seal of Approval of N.A.V.H.

RECKLESS SEDUCTION

GWYNNE FORSTER

THORNDIKE PRESS

A part of Gale, Cengage Learning

Detroit • New York • San Francisco • New Haven, Conn • Waterville, Maine • London

GALE
CENGAGE Learning·

LIBRARY OF CONGRESS CATALOGING-IN-PUBLICATION DATA

Forster, Gwynne.
  Reckless seduction / by Gwynne Forster. — Large print ed.
    p. cm. — (Thorndike Press large print African-American)
  ISBN-13: 978-1-4104-4469-1 (hardcover)
  ISBN-10: 1-4104-4469-4 (hardcover)
    1. African Americans—Fiction. 2. Love stories. gsafd 3. Large type books. I. Title.
  PS3556.O742R43 2012
  813'.54—dc23   2011048692

Published in 2012 by arrangement with Harlequin Books S.A.

Printed in Mexico
1 2 3 4 5 6 7 16 15 14 13 12

My sincere thanks to my
beloved husband and stepson
for their unfailing support
and encouragement.

CHAPTER 1

Haley Feldon stepped out into the late summer sun, grateful for the trees that shaded New York City's East Sixty-Fourth Street. She both loved and hated New York City, but if her dreams were ever to have the slightest chance of materializing, it was where she had to be.

She'd had a difficult meeting with Tom Brennan, one of her backers, that morning. The conceited old coot never missed an opportunity to remind her of his wealth or to mention his generous contributions to the numerous foundations that depended upon him and others like him to finance their philanthropic work.

As she walked swiftly down Second Avenue, Haley sighed. She hated having to work with Brennan, but their meetings were unavoidable. As founder and president of the International Institute for Social Progress (IISP), she devoted herself to projects that improved the lives of poor women and children. Her immediate goals were to improve educational opportunities for children living on reservations and to establish a program to reduce pregnancies and school dropouts among teenage girls in New York City.

She was determined to make a difference. Unfortunately, her work brought her into contact with men like Brennan, because making a difference cost money. And funding for projects like the ones she envisioned for IISP was hard to come by.

Haley glanced at her watch and saw that she had about an hour before her appointment with Nedia Edstrom, head of the United Nations Conference on Social Change. That would give her time for coffee and a few minutes to focus on the proposal that she was presenting to Nedia. Inside the United Nations Secretariat Building, she took the escalator to the second floor and walked down the heavily carpeted corridor toward the North Delegates Lounge. Walking toward her was the tall, sandy-haired man she seemed to glimpse almost every time she came into the Secretariat Building. Elegant and well-built, he exuded an aura of power, strength and pure animal magnetism.

Her response to him always astonished her. How could she react this way to a man she had not even met? Haley was sure that he had his share of female admirers, but she was definitely not going to become one of them. She vowed she wouldn't even though, or perhaps because, he showed up regularly in her dreams and often interfered with her daytime thoughts, too. No, she didn't fool herself. She was acutely aware of him, even if she always tried to pretend that she wasn't. It had gotten so bad that she looked for him every time she entered the building. And she knew that she flushed whenever she saw him. What was it about him? she wondered.

Not to mention she'd caught him looking at her on numerous occasions. She'd always looked away before their gazes could connect. In spite of her natural reserve, she almost hungered to know him. Yet, because she sensed that he represented a danger to her, she usually avoided him. But she wouldn't be able to avoid him today — not this time. Today, he was walking directly to her.

Jon Stig Ecklund leaned back in the chair in his office in the United Nations Secretariat Building. The main office of Ecklund International Syndicate, Inc. (EIS), his family's international satellite network, occupied three floors of a large building on Madison Avenue. Jon preferred to use this smaller office at the UN when he needed privacy or solitude for his work.

He didn't enjoy being alone, but sometimes he needed absolute quiet to hear himself think. Yet even in the solitude of this smaller office Jon was finding it hard to concentrate today. He pushed back his chair, walked out of the office and headed to the North Delegates Lounge for a drink and a break. He took the escalator to the second floor and started for the lounge. It was then that he saw her.

He had seen her at a distance so many times that he felt as if he knew her. Actually, he did know her, because she had spent many hours in his dreams. Her beauty intrigued him. Her regal bearing, long jet-black hair, olive complexion and soft brown eyes bespoke of mixed heritage. And with her tall, perfectly proportioned figure and lovely face she could have been a fashion model. Yet he knew instinctively that there was more to her than beauty. He'd once seen her in the dignified Delegates Dining Room daintily plucking raspberries from her plate and eating them one by one with

10

her fingers. He guessed that she was at once respectable and sassy. She exuded calm coolness, yet Jon wondered if she hid fiery passion beneath her cold facade. He was drawn to her like a moth to fire.

Dammit, he wanted to *know* her. But she never gave him the opportunity. Every time he managed to get close enough to speak to her, she bolted like a skittish colt. He was fast losing patience with that game. She was an enigma that he was going to solve . . . and then forget.

Haley wanted to turn around and go the other way, but it was too late. He was looking directly at her, and her usual calm deserted her. He was handsome. No, he was beautiful. And he was tall, maybe six feet four or five inches. Not many men towered over her, but his height dwarfed her five-ten frame. So this is how dainty felt, Haley thought.

He seemed to pause in his approach. Was he going to speak? She realized she'd never heard his voice. Now she was dying to know if his voice matched his smooth masculine good looks.

Jon held her gaze until he was abreast of her. "Good morning." He said it softly, as if not to frighten her, but she didn't respond.

11

She saw him open his mouth, and in an act of uncharacteristic cowardliness, she glanced away. The moment passed. She wasn't sure whether she walked faster or slower, but when she passed through the lounge and reached the coffee shop, she had strength only to find a table and sit down. She hugged her stomach, calming herself. She knew something else about him now. He had blond hair and long eyelashes that half hid a pair of piercing, fern-green eyes — beautiful eyes. She wanted to kick herself for not speaking to him.

Resuming his normally brisk stride, Jon promised himself that no matter where he saw her again or who she was with, he was going to speak to her. The thought that he would finally settle something that was definitely getting out of hand lightened his mood.

He walked on, mulling over his encounter with the woman. Who the hell was she? What was it about her, a woman of whom he knew absolutely nothing, that made him feel so empty, so lacking in something that he could not label but that was so vital it gnawed at him? He released a long sigh. He wanted her out of his thoughts, out of his mind. He didn't need this aggravation, this teenage craving for something he shouldn't want and couldn't get. Having given himself that stern lecture, he quickened his steps to the lounge. He'd have a vodka.

"Haley Feldon! Haven't seen you in ages. How's the institute going? I heard that you'd delivered a first-class lecture down on Capitol Hill. Do you think you stand a chance of introducing some new life into the secondary school programs for Native American children on reservations? Can I get you an espresso?"

Haley's face creased into a big smile at the sight of her old friend. "Hello, Nels. It's good to see you. How is Isabella? Are you two still an item? And yes, I'd love an espresso." *And thank you for distracting me, bringing me back to earth.*

"Say, why were you sitting with your back to the entrance? Are you hiding from someone?"

Before she could answer, she heard Nels call out to someone. "Jon Ecklund, where have you been? Come over here and join us." Haley felt the hair prickle on the back of her neck.

"Nels Andersen, son of a gun, you're a sight for sore ey . . . Well! Hello, at last."

Haley knew who it was even before she

looked up.

"Hello." Was that dry quivering voice hers? Did they notice how it trembled?

"Have you two met?" Nels asked, rather tentatively.

"We have now," Jon offered. "Who *are* you?" He looked at her intently.

"I'm Haley Feldon," she said, extending her hand. He took it and held it, still looking at her. She felt the blood warm the skin of her face and experienced something that she had never felt before, a flash of warmth from head to foot, the heat settling in the pit of her loins. She hated that she had reacted to him that way. Withdrawing her hand, she took refuge in the lukewarm espresso. It was a mistake. Her hand shook as she raised the cup to her lips, and both men saw it.

"I've got exactly nine minutes to make an appointment on the twenty-second floor. It was a pleasant surprise seeing you, Nels. I wish I had more time. Perhaps we can get together for lunch one of these days. Goodbye, Mr. Ecklund."

"Aren't you implying that you aren't pleased to have met me?" Jon asked, sardonically. He had the pleasure of seeing her speechless. But she quickly regained her composure, smiled rather lamely and hurriedly walked away.

"What on earth is going on between you two?" Nels wanted to know.

"Nothing! Absolutely nothing!"

"Is there anything I can do to help this 'nothing' along?" Nels asked. "You know I'm always willing to do anything I can for a college buddy."

"No! If there's anything I don't need, Nels, it's the kind of chaos you can create when you start your pranks. I'm not in the market for a woman. And if I was, I'd look for one a bit warmer than that porcelain Venus."

Few people knew that second side of Nels's personality, and most anyone would have had difficulty reconciling the boyish prankster with the suave, efficient journalist, the tough adversary that aptly characterized Nels Andersen.

Nels lifted his right shoulder in a careless shrug. "Well, at least you admit that she's a goddess. Haley is a wonderful human being, but I thought I caught some sparks between you two."

"Look, Nels, drop it! Just drop it, will you? A lot of things have happened since we last saw each other. My divorce is final. Karen has remarried, and I'm not looking for anybody." No, he wasn't looking, but that

15

didn't mean that he didn't want Haley Feldon. At least he wanted to get to know her, find out whether . . . What the hell *did* he want?

Nels watched Jon carefully. There was something different there. He was guarded, where he had always been so open, direct and straightforward. He wondered about Jon's divorce. Well, he thought, Jon had always been somewhat reticent with women, though they sure as hell liked him. Maybe someday they'd be able to talk about it. Nels considered it for a moment. He had never given any thought to pranks with Jon where women were concerned. Somewhat bemused at his thoughts, he realized that he never would. For all his apparent toughness, Jon was too vulnerable.

"Look, man, I'm inviting some of the old gang over in a couple of weeks, after I get back from my assignment in Eastern Europe. As soon as I finalize my plans, you know . . . guest list and all that, I'll call you. Will you come?"

"Sure," Jon said, frowning slightly as he gave Nels his home phone number.

Nels rose and patted Jon on the shoulder. "Let's stay in touch, buddy," he said softly, giving Jon his number.

"By the way, Nels, why is it that you aren't

16

interested in Ms. Feldon?"

Nels laughed. "It's *Dr.* Feldon. I knew her when she didn't have all of that polish," he said, cryptically.

"What *ever* do you mean?"

"Well, I covered Peace Corps activities in Africa and used to see her in Kenya. She was just an idealistic kid back then. She's still idealistic."

"Well, she's certainly no kid now," Jon drawled. "See you."

Haley fastened her seat belt and prepared for the sixteen-hour flight to Nairobi. She was pleased with the contract that she had negotiated for IISP with Nedia and had spent the past ten days developing the material for the seminars and workshops that were intended to aid the improvement of women's health in several East African countries. This was what she had dreamed of for her institute.

Owing to the negligence of one of her senior staff members, she'd been up until two in the morning completing preparations for her trip. She'd had enough of him and intended to fire him as soon as she found a replacement. Feeling immensely relieved for having come to that decision, she signaled the stewardess and asked for a cocktail, got out a novel by her favorite writer and settled down. It would be good to see Nairobi again after five years.

At about page twenty in the book, she realized that she'd only been looking at the words while seeing the face of Jon Ecklund. Sure, he'd made an impression on her. Every time she saw him, she'd become conscious of herself as a woman. Something about him drew her like a magnet draws a nail, and she didn't find that soothing. She didn't intend to give another man the power to make her need him and then to humiliate her. After four years, she was still tormented by that experience. No matter how elegant her appearance, how many admiring looks she received and how successful she was professionally, she had only to remember Joshua Hines and his bigoted parents to have her self-confidence shaken and her ego shattered.

Not even the fact that Jon Ecklund seemed attracted to her helped. After all, Josh had claimed to be crazy about her. But his parents — both of whom claimed to have ancestors who came to Plymouth, Massachusetts, on the Mayflower — didn't want him with a black woman. And for all his seemingly tough exterior, Josh proved to be as spineless as a shrimp.

How could she have been such a fool? She wished to God that she had never seen Josh. And if she could, she'd put two continents between herself and Jon Ecklund.

He isn't my problem, I am. He probably hasn't given me another thought, she thought to herself and smiled.

Haley's seatmate on the London-Nairobi leg of the trip was a distinguished-looking man about fifty years old. She attempted to discourage conversation with him, but he would not be denied. When he produced pictures of his family, on whom he clearly doted, she relaxed and became friendlier. Edgar Layton was a London-based entrepreneur, movie producer and sportsman who knew his way around East Africa and a good deal of the rest of the world. He and his family would be spending the winter at their home in Nairobi. When he learned of Haley's mission, he assured her that she had only to call his Nairobi office and he would arrange for as much press coverage as she needed and introduce her to any official who could make her work easier.

Layton proved to be as good as his word. And when Haley's local counterpart failed to keep the first day's appointment, leaving her effectively stranded, she called him and, within an hour, was able to begin her work.

He also invited her to dinner at his home the following evening.

She dressed for the dinner in pink silk slacks and a shirt of matching fabric and color. Layton had said that dining tended to be casual. She found there a very congenial group of expatriates, including Layton's American-born wife, whom she liked immediately. But the surprise, and she wasn't sure whether it was a welcome one, was meeting Ian MacKenlin, head of Ecklund International Syndicate's regional bureau. *Dear God. She was thousands of miles from him, but she hadn't escaped him.* When Ian learned of her project, he let her know at once that EIS was at her disposal for press and publicity. *What would he say if he knew that she couldn't get his boss out of her head?*

Jon stopped by Ida's Gourmet Takeout on First Avenue, bought his dinner and headed home. He wanted to catch the seven o'clock international news roundup on EIS TV. He set the containers of crab cakes, red potato salad with dill and sour cream and green beans with butter-almond sauce on his coffee table, opened a can of beer, kicked off his shoes and settled in for dinner and news. He couldn't believe his eyes when Haley appeared on his screen, explaining the importance of diet, clean water, sanitation and prenatal care for pregnant women. He listened spellbound while she outlined a number of simple and inexpensive measures that would reduce the high risk of childbirth for East African women. And he learned that she would spend two weeks there training social and health workers.

Well, well, he thought, so Dr. Feldon knew her stuff. And she looked damned good on camera, too. She wore that shade of pink well, but to his taste that color was too virginal. The clip was short, but he supposed Ian gave her as much time as he could. He'd like to know more about her, and he made a mental note to call her office the next day.

Amy, Haley's secretary, was too delighted to outline Haley's mission for Jon. It didn't escape him that, given the slightest bit of encouragement, she would have produced a litany of her boss's virtues. As it was, she didn't use much self-restraint, informing him that Haley was successful because she devoted all of her time to work and practically none to social life and relaxation. Jon wondered why she needed to tell him that. He respected intelligence and hard work in anybody, but he'd never admired workaholics. Somehow he didn't think that Haley Feldon's life was as unbalanced as her

21

secretary's description suggested. He didn't question his pleasure at learning that Haley evidently wasn't spending a lot of time with a man.

Nels paced the balcony of his river view apartment on the Upper East Side. Where were they? He'd gone to considerable inconvenience to arrange an opportunity for Jon and Haley to get together in circumstances more conducive to developing a friendship than chance encounters at the United Nations coffee shop. A glance at his watch told him that it was after nine o'clock. Both were usually good as their word. At last, the doorbell rang. He went to the door, opened it and he watched Haley enter. She looked great as usual. She had changed since they knew each other years earlier, but he couldn't put a finger on it. Was it polish or sadness?

"There you are," he beamed. "Come over here. I want you to meet some friends." He hadn't meant for Art Chasen to be the first person she met there. Art was definitely not the man you introduced to your sister or to any woman you admired. He needn't have worried. Haley appraised Art coolly, politely, but kept walking.

"I can see that you've grown up," he told

her with brotherly affection. "You couldn't have dusted Art off more effectively if you had used a chamois."

"Nels, I don't play games with men. I want everything up front. It's easier that way, and one is less likely to get hurt."

"Someone hurt you, Haley?" Nels regarded her closely. Was he doing the right thing, getting these two wounded doves together?

"Let us just say that I have learned the value of caution," she said.

"Caution about what?" Haley pivoted around at the sound of Jon's voice. Why hadn't she suspected that Nels would invite *him?* She wasn't prepared for this. Why was she lying to herself? She was prepared for it. Hadn't she changed dresses three times before settling on a figure-revealing burnt-orange silk shift, hoping that Jon would be there?

Neither she nor Nels answered.

"My, but you are elegant, as usual," Jon added. "You're very lovely tonight, Dr. Feldon."

"Thank you, and please call me Haley. Dr. Feldon is so formal and seems out of place at the party of a mutual friend."

"I'll let you two get better acquainted," Nels said and walked away. There was a moment of awkward silence.

"Will you call me Jon?"

Haley was startled by the question. Even so, she decided that she liked his voice. Deep and resonant, it befitted the big man that he was, and like the rest of him, it had nothing to spare . . . Crisp, with just a touch of lilt. He wore a dark gray suit, pale gray on gray silk shirt and a yellow tie almost the color of his hair. She looked at him. He stood no more than an inch taller than Nels, yet beside him, she felt small and feminine. Nels made her feel nothing but friendship.

Her gaze roamed over the lean, beautifully structured form of him, lingering on his muscular thighs, his broad shoulders and, finally, lifting to his mouth. Dear Lord. *His mouth!* It was the most sensuous thing she had ever seen. Unable to stop herself, she finally, if unwillingly, looked into his fern-green eyes and gasped, audibly. Those green eyes blazed with blatant desire, obviously triggered by her appraisal of him. She looked first at the floor and then toward the ceiling — anyplace but at him.

"Have you eaten?" he asked, attempting to put her at ease.

"No, I haven't. Thank you."

Splaying his fingers at her lower back, he guided her to the buffet table of hors d'oeuvres. Somewhat wobbly from their visual caress, she was grateful for his support. He handed her a finger sandwich of smoked salmon, cream cheese and dill on pumpernickel and seemed fascinated as she managed to nibble it without touching her lips. He dipped a crab claw in some pink dressing and then into his mouth.

"Mmm, but this is good," he said gazing at her. He cleaned his top lip with the tip of his tongue. She knew he hadn't meant to be provocative, but that gesture was the epitome of provocation.

She stared at him. Was his every move a sexual innuendo? Maybe she was just reading sensuality into it. In all her twenty-eight years, she had never responded to a man this way. She probably didn't even know what a woman's response to a man was supposed to be. Lord knows, her one short abysmal experience with Joshua had been devastating.

"The annual Second Avenue festival starts Friday. Have you ever been?" At this point, she would've said anything to change the focus of her unruly thoughts.

"No. Why?" he asked.

"You seem to enjoy eating, and some of the food at that festival is so fantastic that I just throw caution to the four winds, forget the guilt and dig in."

Jon sensed that she wanted to find neutral ground, that the electricity passing between them had made her uneasy. But he'd be damned if he was going to chitchat about something so banal as a street fair. He'd choose his own safe topic.

"You were great on camera," he said. "You looked good, too. After I recovered from the surprise of seeing you, I listened to what you had to say. Your message was impressive. If you ever want to change careers, I hope you'll consider EIS. Believe me, the door is open."

She made no effort to hide her pleasure at his remarks. "Thank you," she said, simply. "I was a little nervous, as I'd had less than an hour's notice that my talk would be televised. And I was excited when I realized that it would be broadcast to the States." *And that it was your network and that you would probably see me,* she added silently.

"What do you think of Ian MacKenlin?" Now, why had he asked that? What could she think? Ian was competent and always did his job well. He was also hell with women or had been before he married the year before. What was it to him, anyway? What she did was her business. He made an effort to straighten out his mind and get it going in the right direction. He hardly knew this woman, and it was foolish to be thinking about what man she'd seen or hadn't seen, liked or hadn't liked. "Did he, uh, show you around, some sightseeing, that sort of thing?" He winced at his own transparency.

"Why? Is that company policy?"

"Well, for someone who's never been to the place before . . ." He stopped himself. He wouldn't continue that inane conversation. And what she did, he reminded himself again, was her business. Still . . .

"Mr. MacKenlin introduced me to his wife, who took me shopping in the local marketplace and on home to dinner with them. It was a wonderful evening, and I'm hoping that she and I will remain friends, even over long distance." She wondered why Jon Ecklund was asking her about Mac-Kenlin. Could he possibly care who she was with? Her mind wondered on. She'd bet her PhD that Jon Ecklund was a thorough man. Thinking that if he made love to a woman, he'd do a man's job of it, she felt her mouth go dry and her face heat up. She tried not to look at him, but her eyes disobeyed her, and she stared into those fern-green pools of sensuality. God help her, she didn't want this.

"Do you like music?" he asked, bringing her out of her reverie.

"Yes," she said. He had rescued her again. "I like the classics, especially Mozart, most of Puccini's operas, blues and classical jazz. I love jazz."

He listened to her low, soft voice. It warmed him. Yes, just being with her warmed him. Maybe she wasn't as cold as she always looked. He took her hand, and although she offered no objection, he sensed the tension in her.

"Will you dance with me?" He wanted her in his arms. He knew that he should go slowly, but he couldn't. His instinct told him that he was vulnerable to her, but he pushed the warning aside. "Come with me," he said softly, her hand still wrapped in his. She said nothing and didn't remove her hand, but she went with him.

Nels had converted the dining room for dancing, and several couples were on the floor. As the band began to play "If I Loved You" from Nels's sound system, he turned to her and opened his arms. She walked into them. For seconds, they didn't move. Then he began a slow two-step. Though she was tall, at least five feet ten inches, he had to bend a little. She reached up and put her arms around his neck, as if in an embrace and, as he moved, she began to sing the words in a sweet, sultry contralto. She had him spellbound. Her beautiful voice reached into his heart and grabbed him, and her soft body molded perfectly to his. He knew he should put on the brakes, but he wanted more. He didn't know where it would lead, but he wanted to know her, all of her.

They realized that the music had stopped and that they still held each other.

"You must be a magician."

"Who, me?" He couldn't believe that anyone would describe him in that manner.

"Yes, you," she bantered. "You've cast a spell on me. I don't hug strange men," she continued, laughing. He grinned. Then he laughed a clear, soul-cleansing laugh.

She stared at him, captivated. "You ought to laugh all the time," she blurted out. "You're very attractive when you laugh."

He stopped laughing and just looked at her. Was she making a pass at him? She was dead serious. She thought he was good looking, at least when he laughed.

"Keep me happy, and I'll laugh all you want."

She didn't respond.

"I was jesting, Haley, I don't mean to step

out of line with you," he said softly.

"Step out of line? I thought you were being witty. What does it take to keep you happy? I can imagine that you don't want for the company of beautiful women." They walked off the floor, but the closeness that they had felt was gone.

He thought for a moment. He wanted to be truthful without seeming arrogant. "Beautiful, sophisticated women are not what it takes to make me happy or, for that matter, even to alleviate boredom."

When she didn't respond, he asked himself how they had gotten into something that personal. She had been teasing, and his response had been way too serious.

Nels rescued them. "I see you two have been getting acquainted. Supper is being served. Come on back in the kitchen. I've set a table for the three of us back there."

"Are you deserting your other guests, Nels?" Haley wanted to know.

Nels grinned, effectively admitting that he was matchmaking. "The only guests of importance are right here with me. I see the rest of them as often as I like. Let's plan a time when we can get together, Jon. I want to know what you've been doing these past five years."

"Okay, we'll plan something." They bantered and joked as if they had always been a threesome. When they'd finished the roasted pheasant, grilled mushrooms and steamed artichokes, they had a green salad and Blue Stilton cheese.

Haley leaned back and sighed. "Nels, if I had a butler, I'd want you to train him. You're the perfect host."

"He is, if he happens to want to pick your brain, like now," Jon observed.

After raspberry sherbet and coffee, Jon stood. "It's time to call this wonderful evening to a halt. May I see you home, Haley?"

"Oh, I live way over on the west side."

"*Where* on the west side?" Jon asked her.

"Well, Riverside Drive. That's probably out of your way." It was twenty-five blocks out of his way, if he was concerned with distance. But his instincts told him that it was the most direct route to where he wanted to be.

"No, it isn't out of my way. I'll give you a call, Nels."

Haley hugged Nels and thanked him for the party, and it annoyed Jon that she put her arms around Nels and kissed him on the cheek. He refused to ask himself why he should get sore about a thing like that.

"Shape up, man," he said to himself. She

didn't belong to him and never would. What had he been thinking all evening, anyway? As they reached the elevator, he felt himself withdrawing.

They were silent as the elevator descended the twenty-two floors to the lobby. She didn't look at Jon, but he looked at her. Why hadn't he told Nels that he'd be busy? He'd had a suspicion that she would be there. Damn, he'd wanted her to be there, had wanted to see her again. He knew that she sensed his withdrawal and was hurt by it, but he made no move to bridge the chasm that he had deliberately erected between them. He was never going to give another woman the opportunity to crush him — and that included the elegant Dr. Feldon.

As they reached the street, Haley sighted a taxi, flagged it and reached for its door.

"Now, wait a minute, here. I told you that I would see you home."

"No, thank you. I am perfectly capable of seeing myself safely home, and I won't have to contend with any lightning fast mood changes, since I don't have them." She closed the door and gave the cabbie her address. The taxi moved away from the curb, leaving a stunned Jon staring at its taillights. No goodbye, no see you, no nothing. Well, what should he have expected?

"You young people are always quarreling. Now, me and my Beth, we never had a cross word from the time we met, and we've been married forty-three years. Soon as I set eyes on 'er, I knew she was for me. Your man seemed like a nice one," the cabbie said. "What's the problem? Think you two can work it out?"

Haley blew out a long breath. "The trouble with him is that he goes from tepid to hot to cold in a couple of minutes, and I like dependable personalities and stability in my life. Anyway, he isn't my man."

"From what you just said, I can tell he's 'bout hooked. You listen to me, here. When a man acts like that, he's interested — don't want to be and fast losing the battle. You'll see. Well, here ya are, little lady. That's thirteen-eighty. Mark my word, you ain't seen the last of that one."

Haley leaned back in her desk chair and let her gaze sweep the autumn colors that beautified her office. She'd been in that rut ever since Nels's party. Three weeks down the drain. If she didn't get that proposal written, she could just forget about the health education program for reservation children. She swore vehemently. Why couldn't she get Jon Ecklund out of her head? She couldn't think of anything except the way she'd felt in his arms when he held her and danced with her. She'd felt his masculine strength, the force of his personality and his barely controlled passion. She knew he wanted her, and she also knew that something restrained him. She told herself that it was best to forget about him. Come hell or high water, she would.

The ring of the telephone invaded her thoughts. "Yes, Amy?" Amy had been her secretary since the doors of IISP first opened. The stunning fifty-year-old red-headed grandmother had a husband who had practically worshipped her for 28 years. She was fiercely loyal to Haley.

"Mr. Andersen. Can you take it?"

"Hello, Nels. What can I do for you?"

"Well, you can begin by being less officious. What in heaven's name have you done to Jon? He came over yesterday, asking all kinds of questions about you. But he didn't want any answers. I think he just wanted to get tanked, and believe me, he got tanked. And he didn't even get high once when we were in college. I still can't believe he did what I saw him do yesterday."

"You were in college with him?"

"Yeah. We were roommates and best friends for four years as undergraduates and two years in graduate school. We both got degrees in journalism. Haley, Jon is about the finest man I have ever met. If I had a sister, I would do my best to make him my brother-in-law. He's straight. And you've got him spinning. We've got to talk about this."

"Nels, I'll talk about anything you want after I finish this grant proposal. I am trying to get funding for a project to improve health education among reservation kids in the first through ninth grades."

"Are we speaking every kid on every reservation?"

"No, I'm just going to try two or three pilot projects, just to demonstrate what can be done with a small investment."

"Are you going to include the Comanche, since they're your own people?"

"Nels, the Comanche do not live on a reservation, though most of us are settled out in Oklahoma."

"Haley, I'm not about to go into the geography of the Native Americans right now. I want to talk to you about Jon."

"Nels, give me a break. I don't want to talk about Jon Ecklund. Period. That man is the reason why I'm struggling with this proposal and getting nowhere."

"Why, what did he do?"

"Nothing" was the nettled response. She said goodbye and placed the phone in its cradle. It was enough to have to think about the man; she'd be damned if she was going to spend the afternoon talking about him. Besides, anybody with sense could see that Jon Ecklund was more than man enough to fight his own battles and win his own wars.

What I need, she thought, after a moment of reflection, is better information about the schools on these reservations. She punched the intercom button. "Amy, please tell Spencer that I want to see him *now.*"

"Right, Haley."

"Spencer, I want a report on the national ranking of primary and secondary students attending school on these three reservations — students per teacher, average attendance and annual education expenditure per student. And I want it by ten o'clock tomorrow morning."

"You don't want much," a chastened Spencer observed.

"No, I don't. See you at ten o'clock in the morning." As Spencer walked out, it occurred to her that she would probably fire him within the next six months. His arrogance was becoming intolerable.

Maybe she should make on-site visits to the schools, using Spencer's report as preparatory material. Where was she going to get all of this time? Her mother might have some ideas. Haley telephoned her in Washington, and indeed she did. Gale Feldon had taken early retirement from her university post as professor of history, but retirement didn't sit well with her. Haley wasn't surprised when her mother offered to make the trip out to Oklahoma and undertake an on-site investigation. Unlike her daughter, Gale understood and spoke the language and had good contacts among her own people. That was all the entrée she would need to speak to the neighboring tribes. They agreed that she and Gale would leave Wednesday morning, carrying Spencer's report and a consultant's contract from IISP. Haley would visit schools of the other two tribes.

Haley was back in her office the following Monday morning with everything she needed for the proposal. Gale Feldon's highly professional report awaited her. Now, she only had to put it together and polish it off. "Yes, Amy."

"Mr. Ecklund. He's called half a dozen

times since you left on Wednesday. I left the notes on your desk."

"Thanks, I'll take the call. Hello, Jon."

"Hello, Haley." She had forgotten the beauty of his deep, velvet baritone. It warmed her all over. It soothed her, wrapped her up in warm contentment.

"Haley, would you have dinner with me tonight? I want to see you again. Something went wrong between us. Will you please let me clear it up?"

"Jon, I'm terribly busy. I'm sorry."

"Just like that? But you will eat, won't you? I know that I am responsible for the hostility that you must feel toward me, but —"

She interrupted him. It wasn't exactly hostility that she felt toward him, but he had hurt her, and she didn't want to expose herself to any more hurt from him.

"I do not feel hostile toward you. I told you. I'm busy. I have to finish a proposal."

"All right. When will you have dinner with me?"

"If I agree to have dinner with you, are you sure you won't change your mind, lose your appetite, get an urgent call to leave town or something?"

"I deserve that."

"My, my, such humility. I have to get back

38

to work now. Goodbye." She hung up.

"Amy, come in and take a letter, please." Amy's pleasant smile disappeared abruptly as she walked into the office, and from her demeanor, Haley knew that Amy had detected her distress.

"This is to the Brayton-Rogers Foundation. The usual salutation. I am writing to request your support of educa . . ." She couldn't stop the tremors in her voice. Horrified, Amy moved forward to comfort her, but embarrassed, Haley stepped away from the desk.

"Amy, please excuse me for a few minutes."

"But, Haley —"

"I'll be fine. Please, Amy."

Amy left. Haley went into her private bathroom and calmed herself. She hadn't wanted to hurt Jon, only to preserve her sanity. How must he feel? She had never hung up on anybody, not even people whom she disliked. Why had she reacted so harshly?

When she had regained composure, she acknowledged to herself that she should apologize to Jon. After looking through her personal address book, she dialed a number from it. Nels answered on the first ring.

"Haley here. Can you give me Jon's telephone number?"

"Home or office?"

"Wherever he's likely to be right now."

He gave her both. "Haley, what is going on?"

She thought for a moment. "Nels, I really don't know. Please be a friend, and don't ask anything of me just now."

"Alright, love, but be careful. He's had a few serious wounds. Best of luck."

I've had some bad scratches myself, she thought, as she dialed Jon's number.

"Ecklund." He couldn't know that the sound of his voice disarmed her.

"Yes." He spoke sharply.

"Jon, this is Haley."

"Yes, Haley? I was leaving my office when the phone rang. What is it?"

"I'm extremely sorry about my rudeness." She realized she sounded stiff and formal. "I . . . I just panicked. I've never done such a thing before."

"Is the fact that you've given me this singular honor supposed to soothe my ego?" he asked, his tone as bitter as his words.

"Please don't hold it against me."

"What prompted it, Haley? Frankly, I was shocked."

He wasn't going to help, and she didn't blame him. "I called because I would never deliberately attempt to hurt you. I confess that my reaction to you confuses me."

"Why should you panic? Because you're accustomed to being in control, and you're not? Well, neither one of us is. Look, I'd settle for some honesty between us. You were honest when you danced with me that night at Nels's party. But because I didn't know where I was headed and showed it, I earned your displeasure and perhaps your distrust. I called you today to put it right. The ball is in your court now. I want to know you better, but crawling is not something that I do."

"We could have dinner together tomorrow night." Had she said that? She knew that she would regret it. She could never be indifferent to this man. And yet she could not — would not — open herself to the possibility of another demoralizing intimacy.

"What about that urgent proposal?"

"Dinner with you may be just what's needed to expedite it," she said, cryptically.

Jon pondered that for a bit.

"I'll call for you at seven-thirty." She hadn't given him her address, but he'd get it just like she got his telephone number — from Nels.

He leaned forward, elbows on his desk, hands together and fingers spread pyramid

41

fashion. Why had he agreed to that date? When he'd heard her voice, he'd felt a yearning for her that he hadn't had for a woman in years. He'd been alone by choice for five years, forcing himself not to want, not to need. But she made him want, made him need, made him ache. He hungered for her. He'd suspected that her cool composure was a farce, a facade, a cover for the softness that she had unwittingly displayed in unguarded moments when they danced.

One thing was certain: Haley Feldon did not want to be soft or passionate. She was trying to project an image of being cool, tough and unattainable. He'd have dinner with her, yes, but he'd be damned if he was going to be sucked into a quicksand of emotion.

He closed his eyes, and the vision of her floated before him. He could see her doe-soft, beguiling brown eyes, and he shuddered. Hell, what he needed was fifty laps in his upstate pool.

"Ecklund, you're losing it," he said aloud. But his spirits buoyed for reasons that he didn't bother to examine. He left his office whistling "If I Loved You."

CHAPTER 2

Haley dressed in a strapless antique-gold silk dress that revealed just enough cleavage to make a man's mouth water. She carried the matching jacket on her arm. Jon arrived precisely at seven-thirty, and when she opened the door, they stared at each other. He recovered first.

"Hello, Haley. You seem more beautiful tonight than ever." He was not sure how she would react to his comment or what she wanted of him. But she had certainly dressed in a way that pleased him.

"Welcome to my home, Jon. You look wonderful," she said, mostly because she was nervous. And so he did. He wore a tan summer suit, beige silk shirt, a burnt-orange-and-brown-striped tie and brown Gucci loafers. She'd never found blond men attractive, but this one was something special. He was the quintessential male — strong, sensual and controlled. Jon personified virility. And his mouth, with the full bottom lip, was his best feature.

"May I come in?"

She realized she'd been staring again.

"Oh, I'm sorry." She stepped aside, and he walked in a few paces. Then without knowing that he would, he stopped in front of her, a breath away. She looked up at him, wide-eyed and a little frightened.

Jon told himself to use some judgment and move away. But he hadn't realized how badly he'd wanted to see her, to be with her, to hold her. He touched her cheek with his thumb. She didn't move. He ran his thumb back and forth over her lower lip. She didn't move. He pulled her into his arms, lowered his head and took her mouth. Was he dreaming or what? She had her arms around his neck, her fingers were in his hair and her lips were moving beneath his. He wanted more and asked for it, offering her his tongue. She parted her lips, pulled it into her mouth and gently sucked it.

Sensing that he was about to lose control altogether, abruptly he sought to break the kiss, not wanting to expose his need for her. He didn't want her to feel the indisputable evidence of it. But she wouldn't let him go, holding him to her until the shocking force of his physical desire against her belly restored her presence of mind. They broke apart. He braced both hands against the wall above her head, needing the support and simultaneously trapping her between him and the wall. From hooded eyes, he looked at a spot just over her shoulder. She drew a deep breath, preparing to speak, but he stopped her.

"Haley, don't tell me that you don't want to see me, that you don't want to spend time with me. I don't want to hear it."

"Jon, I . . . I don't know —"

He interrupted. "What don't you know? Woman, you damned near devoured me just now. At least acknowledge that you want me just as much as I want you."

"Yes," she whispered.

"All right." He touched her nose lightly with one finger and then smiled down at her. "Let's go. We need to get out of here." She stood there, observing him intently, as if seeing him for the first time.

"What is it?" he demanded softly.

"That's the first time I've seen you smile. You grinned once, and I think you laughed once, too. But you've never just smiled." He was devastating when he let that smile light his face. His mouth softened, became even more sensuous and inviting. The sparkles in his fern-green eyes warmed her all over.

45

She let him see her sweetness then, her softness, and the primal female in her. And she didn't bother to hide the fact that when she looked at him she liked what she saw.

Jon had chosen an Italian restaurant with a quiet, attractive ambience. Their dinner was pleasant but uneventful. They hardly spoke to each other, and they barely ate. Both were overwhelmed by their unexpected feelings, and both were wary. They left the restaurant in silence. When they reached his car, he put an arm around her shoulder.

"When will I see you again?" he softly whispered against her ear.

She hesitated.

"Is there a man to whom you are in any way obligated or committed?"

"There is no one else."

His heartbeat accelerated. Her answer suggested that he was a man in her life. "Haley, I have been divorced for five years. It was a painful marriage. I still don't know whether I can face loving and the intimacy it implies ever again." He paused for a long while. She waited patiently for him to continue, but in her eyes, he saw fear.

"Until tonight, I had thought that you and I were probably incompatible. Now, I'm not so sure. Do you want to know whether what

46

we experienced back there at your front door means anything? Whether we really could have something magical? Would you try to learn who and what I am and teach me who and what you are? If you don't want that, then just say so. We'll have spent a pleasant evening, and we'll say goodbye."

She measured her words carefully. "If you're willing to go slowly, if you will be patient . . . I want to try. It won't be easy for me."

"Nor for me."

He brushed her cheek lightly with his knuckle. "Whatever happens between us, Haley, please be honest with me. That's all I'm asking right now." She hugged him quickly and released him.

He raised one eyebrow quizzically in response.

"You asked for honesty. That was some honesty," she said.

Laughing, he tucked her into the car, took her home and left her at her front door.

Had she really hugged him spontaneously like that? Jon lay in his bed, the room lit only by the stars. He was ordinarily a man who went to sleep when sleep was what he wanted. But on this night, sleep was elusive, waylaid by his visions of her. He wanted to

47

believe that he could find true union with her. He knew that she was strongly attracted to him, but she had given him no reason to think that she possessed the compassion that would bring him the sweet communion that he had yearned for all of his adult life. Could he risk it? Hadn't he promised himself that he would never again allow himself to need another woman? Hadn't he had enough experience with the consequence of such folly? At half past three in the morning, he left his bed, showered, dressed, got in his car and went to his Madison Avenue office. At least he could catch MacKenlin out in Nairobi, where it was already just after ten o'clock.

"Hello, Ian, Jon Ecklund, here. You've been difficult to reach. Any problems?"

"Morning, Jon, I've been over in Sortundi. There are problems, yes, but not the kind you have in mind. Half of the developed countries in the world are sending food and medicine to the sick and hungry in northeastern Africa, but most of it isn't getting through."

"Why not?"

"Well, as far as I can judge, there's politics, bureaucratic bungling, indifference on the part of officials, plain incompetence and just about any other obstacle you care to name.

48

My preference is for a story about that rather than about the people who are suffering. That's hardly news."

"It's your story. Get it. If you take pictures, be careful. It could be dangerous. In any case, you've got my support. If you need something, give me a call." As he hung up, it occurred to him that an investigative report of that sort might cause a slackening off of help to that region. Well, needy people weren't getting the help that was being sent anyway. It was his responsibility to see that that fact was known.

He went up to the canteen, put a dollar into the machine and got a cup of dreadful coffee. He sipped it on the way back to his office. Summoning as much discipline as he could muster, he got down to work. By the time Maxine, his secretary, arrived at nine o'clock, Jon had done a day's work. The aroma of good coffee wafting in from her office told him that she had arrived.

He punched the intercom. "Good morning, Maxine. I want to dictate some letters as soon as you get straightened out."

"Morning, Jon. Be right there." She walked in, swaying seductively and bringing him the long-awaited coffee.

49

"Thanks. You make the best coffee, Maxine."

"You must have been working for hours. Couldn't you sleep last night? There's a cure for that."

"Maxine, you're an excellent secretary, but you've been getting a bit too personal with me lately, and I don't like it." He knew she wanted him, and he was getting tired of her innuendos and less and less subtle pressure. "Now, let's get to work." He ignored her pouting and made a mental note to put her in another department, away from him. Any involvement with her would be ruinous to him, not that he was tempted. He wasn't. Only Haley Feldon had interested him in any way in the past five years. He wouldn't think about her, dammit. He had work to do.

Jon sat alone in his office at eight o'clock in the evening. He'd been there over sixteen hours. There was no crisis, no pressing problem that required an urgent solution. So why didn't he leave? He didn't leave because there was only one place that he wanted to be, and he was increasingly ambivalent about giving free rein to his growing feelings for Haley. Since his divorce, work had been his life. He had buried himself in it, had built EIS into a powerful concern. He, his father and their staff could get interviews with heads of state, with the most reclusive celebrity, where other news organizations tried and failed. He had worked hard to build a reputation for honesty, thoroughness and fairness in reporting. His movies and videos were entertaining without relying on violence or graphic sex. He had won several awards. His record, his achievements had been a source of comfort to him, and he had been content with his life.

He realized that he was depressed, a rare occurrence in recent years, and knew that he had to eliminate the source of his dissatisfaction. He left the office and headed home, walking briskly over to Sutton Place. Who was he kidding? His real problem was that he wanted Haley, needed her, but that he hadn't been willing to take the chance. But hadn't he asked for and received her promise to give their relationship a try? Hell, he wasn't a coward. He'd have to risk it. But first he wanted to know what his chances were, what he was up against.

Jon's call so soon after their first date surprised her. She told herself not to act as if his call was unusual.

"Hello, Jon. It's nice to hear from you."

51

"I take it you mean that, so I'm going to ask if we can spend the afternoon together. Can you ride a bicycle?"

"Why yes, but I'd like a rain check on that. Can we do something else? You know . . . walk along Riverside Drive or take a radio and soak up the sun in Central Park. I love being outdoors on a summer Sunday."

"Okay. I'll stop at Grace's Market Place and get a picnic basket, and I should have a bottle of wine here. I'll let you bring the music?"

"What time will you be here?"

"Shortly after twelve. Where do you want to meet?"

"You choose."

He arrived at twelve thirty, minutes after she pressed a pair of white cotton cropped pants, jumped into them and pulled a red T-shirt over her head. "Have you been running?" he asked, having observed her short intakes of breath.

"No, but it took me an hour to find a pair of summer pants, and then I had to iron them."

He raised an eyebrow. "Are you telling me you don't like casual dress?"

"No, I'm not. Everything in its place. I had already stored my summer casuals, thinking that I wouldn't have time to wear them again this summer."

"I'm glad you reconsidered. You look great."

She took the portable CD player and a dozen CDs from the table in the foyer and put them in a shopping bag. He stared at her. "What's the matter?" she asked him.

"I'm enchanted with you. You don't look a bit like the woman I saw all those weeks from afar. You're so much warmer, and you're . . . approachable. Damn, I want to hug you."

"Okay, but none of your heavy duty stuff." She opened her arms, and he walked into them.

"I could definitely get used to this," he said and released her. "Let's go while I can still hold my head up."

"It would be a pity if you got yourself into a situation where your head bobbled around on your neck. Of course, that would merely be a visitation upon you of the sins of your Viking ancestors."

"They got here before Columbus."

"I know. If you want an argument, pick another subject. You have every right to be proud of your heritage."

"You and I have a common heritage. My mother was born in Philadelphia of African American parents, and her skin is just a tiny

53

bit lighter than yours. She straightens her hair or it would be kinkier than mine. She's very beautiful."

"Do you look like her?"

He shook his head, and his eyes twinkled as if he mused over a private joke. "Not one bit. It's accepted that I'm the spitting image of my dad. Svend, my brother, looks just like our mother, except that he's white. He even has black hair. Sometimes we look at each other and laugh about it."

He found a parking space on Eighty-Sixth Street half a block west of Central Park West, got the picnic basket and a cotton blanket from the trunk of his car, took her hand and followed dozens of other New Yorkers into the park.

"Next time, we should bring our bikes, ride over to the lake, rent a canoe and go boating," he said. "I've wanted to do that, but it wouldn't be any fun alone."

She wished that she had agreed to his suggestion that they go bike riding, but she hadn't ridden a bike in years. She told him as much. "If you're willing to start with short trips, we can work up to a long ride."

He spread the blanket beneath an oak tree that offered plenty of shade and stretched out. "Come on. Join me." She hesitated, though she wasn't sure why. He reached up with both arms. "Come on. I won't ravish you. Out here with all these people and in bright daylight, you're as safe as money in Fort Knox."

"Thanks for nothing," she said beneath her breath and sat beside him.

But he let her know that he heard her. "I only promise not to ravish you out here," he said, eased an arm around her waist and let a grin alter the contours of his face.

"You have no idea how much that consoles me, Jon. Imagine me being worried about that!"

He pulled her down to his side. "Don't get me wrong. I wouldn't hesitate to ravish you if we were alone. I don't believe there's a warm-blooded man under sixty who wouldn't do his best to get you into his bed. I'm warm-blooded, and I haven't yet reached sixty."

For a minute, it seemed to her that the breeze blowing over them had heated up, but he turned on his side to face her, and she knew the source of that warmth. His body heat enveloped her like hot quicksand, sucking her into its clutches. He stared into her eyes, and she tried to look away but couldn't.

He stroked her bottom lip with the pad of his index finger. "I've rarely wanted anything as badly as I wanted that kiss," he said. "Maybe if I feed us, we can get our thoughts off each other."

"And you think all it takes is food? You can't be serious."

He shrugged and looked into the distance. "Right now, it's the only option."

She accepted the pastrami on whole wheat sandwich. "I bet if you tried hard you could come up with another one. I mean, the head of EIS is a clever man, isn't he?"

"Listen, you temptress, try to remember not to goad me. I may surprise you."

"Yes, but we've already established that you're a gentleman. You don't beat women, and you want to find out what kind of person I am. Agreed?" He nodded. "In that case, I can be myself. And in case you haven't noticed, I love to flirt."

His eyes widened. Suddenly, he began to laugh. Then the laugh phased into a cough. She slapped him on the back several times.

"Are you all right?" she asked him. "I mean, are you choking?"

He swallowed some wine, cleared his throat and stared at her. "You've got more sides than an octagon, and I want to explore every side and every facet of you."

She thought about that for a long minute. "Then why were you laughing?"

"Frankly, the joke was on me. I realize that in you I might have met my match, and that would be a first."

He poured wine into their glasses and raised his. "I'm going to do everything I can to make you care for me."

She tilted her glass of wine and drank every drop. "At least you have the grace to warn me."

"Seems to me that when you drank that you just gave me license to pull out the stops."

She put her empty glass on the green grass beside her, leaned over and stroked his hair. "I'm counting on your good judgment."

"Be careful, Haley. I've made mistakes, and because I'm still human, I may make some more."

"Not to worry," she said, still stroking. "I'll keep you out of trouble."

"Yeah. Just like you did the other night when we went to dinner." She stretched out beside him, and he needed no further invitation. For the first time, she looked up into his face while lying supine, and frissons of heat plowed through her.

"Kiss me. Open your mouth and kiss me."

She sucked his tongue into her mouth and gripped his shoulders, asking for more, wanting him and relief from the tension stirring in her. Almost immediately, he broke the kiss.

"No more of that." He took her hand and locked her fingers through his. "I haven't felt this content in years. I love being with you, Haley, and I want us to spend as much time as possible together. Can we?"

"I enjoy being with you, Jon, but let's take it one day at a time."

"If that's all you can give me now, I have to accept it. But I want more. Much more."

That night, after wrestling interminably with the sheets on her bed, trying to fit the images of Jon into a safe place outside of her heart, Haley got up and made coffee. Maybe if she worked she'd stop thinking about him. She took her briefcase and files to bed and completed the Brayton-Rogers proposal. She was satisfied that she'd done the best possible job on it. Spencer had produced an excellent report on all three school systems, and her own and her mother's on-site visits had provided material for a first-rate proposal. She went to shower, but as she reached the bathroom, she paused. What was she going to do about Jon?

She'd promised them a chance, but could she risk rejection again? She wanted him.

No, she was crazy for him. In her life, she had never before felt as she had in his arms. He was big, strong and . . . Oh Lord, he was so tender. The way he'd kissed her, hungry, hot, telling her without words that she was desirable. And sweet. He was so sweet and gentle. And he had tried not to let her know what was going on with him, how hard he was. If he'd taken her right there in her foyer, she would probably have let him.

Thank God he hadn't pushed it further. She had thought only about his arms tight around her, his velvet tongue in her mouth and his hard penis pressed against her belly. And when he'd gazed down at her face as she lay on her back in Central Park, letting her see how deeply he felt for her, she had wanted to wrap her arms and legs around him and make love with him.

Later that morning, as she entered her outer office, where Amy sat, she stopped. What on earth was Jon doing here at nine o'clock in the morning?

"Hi." She was disconcerted at seeing him when her mind had been full of him since long before daylight.

"Morning, Haley." He never said good morning or good evening. She loved his low, sonorous baritone, the slow lilting cadence of his speech.

"Come on in," she said, haltingly, not knowing the purpose of his visit and instinctively sensing some kind of a confrontation. Amy brought two mugs of coffee with sugar and cream on the side.

"Mrs. Birch, this is Jon Ecklund. Mr. Ecklund is president and cochairman of Ecklund International Syndicate."

"I'm pleased to meet you in person, Mr. Ecklund. I watch your news channel all the time."

"How do you do, Mrs. Birch?"

Amazed, Haley watched as Jon winked at her secretary.

"I'm delighted that you use our news service. We strive for accurate and comprehensive reporting," he said with a grin.

"That's the impression we all get, too," Amy replied as she left the room smiling. Haley knew that Amy wanted more than anything for her to find a man who would fill the void in her life.

She and Jon gazed at each other quietly, as if words were unnecessary, as if it were enough that they were together. He smiled again, and she felt as if her heart were in her throat. She wondered if he had ever seen himself smile.

"You're ruining my life," he teased. "I can get along without sleep and without food, but it seems I can't go one day without seeing you."

She stared at him.

"And if you don't close your mouth," he went on, "I may have to kiss you."

Was he teasing her?

Rising to the bait, she opened her mouth wider but, filled with mirth, couldn't keep the pose, and a grin broke out over her face. He didn't hesitate — just pulled her out of the chair and hugged her. She looked up at him in wonder, her gaze settling upon his sensuous lips. Then she looked into his eyes and gasped. In that split second, he'd unclothed his soul, and all that he felt, all that he longed for, all that he feared was mirrored in the light of his eyes. She stared, mesmerized, until he bent his head and brushed her lips with his own, ever so lightly, before crushing her mouth with all the longing that she had seen in his eyes. She wrapped her arms around his waist and kissed his cheek.

"I'm going home for six months. Will you be here for me when I get back?"

She pulled away a bit. "When did you decide that?"

"Last night. I have to sort out a lot of

things before I can carry this relationship further. No, there is no other woman and there won't be, but I need to figure some things out."

He needed answers, and he had decided that after all the years of pain and hurt he wanted to be whole. He wasn't giving up this woman without an honest effort to deal with his problem. He would begin with his parents. It had occurred to him that they might have answers. He had always been able to discuss anything with his parents, but he wasn't sure about this.

"Tell me, Haley, do you feel that you can wait for me?"

"I told you that there is no one else. I care for you. Is that enough?"

"It will have to be. Knowing that you care for me means everything." He folded her close to his body. "I'm going to leave tomorrow night. Will you have dinner with me this evening?"

"Yes, I will. How shall I dress? Are you going 'black tie?' "

"Yep." She lifted an eyebrow and nodded assent. She'd been joking, but he clearly had not.

Back at his office, Jon spoke to Maxine through the intercom. "Tell DuPree I want to see him right now."

"Right."

"And, Maxine, I'm transferring you to HR as of this morning. Tell Catherine to send the senior pool secretary to see me in about an hour."

"But, Jon —"

"That will be all, Maxine." He didn't have time for Maxine's brand of male mind bending. She could pout and raise her skirt for the next decade, but he didn't want to put up with it any longer.

"Morning, Jason. I hope I didn't drag you away from something urgent. This is the situation. I'm going to Oslo tomorrow night, possibly for as long as six months, and you'll be in charge here. If there's anything that you need, you know where to call. Any questions?"

Jason DuPree had been with EIS for five years and knew every aspect of its operations. He was also a widely respected journalist and had earned his credentials on the battlefields of Vietnam, as well as AU's School of Journalism. He was a big man physically and wasn't known for tolerating nonsense or disloyalty on the job. He was also a compassionate man who knew how to be a friend.

"Morning, Jon. Yes, you interrupted something. And yes, I have a question."

Jon narrowed his eyes and leaned forward.

"What have you decided to do about Hyfelt?" Dupree asked.

"I'm going to postpone his retirement by sending him over to broadcasting. His scripts will be written for him, as they are for everyone else. He'll have no need to feel as if he's being discriminated against because of his age."

"Couldn't agree with you more. What about Maxine?"

"She's being transferred to human resources after lunch today."

"Excellent idea. I don't like working with her. What about you? Is everything alright with you? I don't mean to pry."

"I'm okay. I'll be working out of the head office during this period. It's just that I need to straighten out a few things back there. I'm glad you're on my team, Jason."

"Me, too. All the best. And keep in touch."

"Will do." Feeling better about his life and his future than he had in years, he cleaned out his desk, left the office and walked out of the building and into the morning sun.

Haley arrived at her Riverside Drive apartment at half past five and wasted no time getting ready for her last evening with Jon.

Six months. She wouldn't see him for six months. She knew that she would miss him, and she also knew that the time was not yet right for their joining as man and woman. He had intimated as much, and she had her own demons to lay to rest. But she refused to allow such thoughts to spoil her time with him that night.

She filled the tub with warm water, dropped in half a cup of French perfumed liquid soap, got her worn copy of Barrett Browning's poems and stepped in for an hour of luxurious self-indulgence.

After her bath, she toweled dry and sprayed her body with perfume. Then she put a pair of red silk bikini panties beneath a red silk chiffon strapless evening gown that hugged her tightly from her bosom to her hip line and then fell straight to her ankles. A slit from the hem to her right thigh completed the daring image. She wore sapphire earrings and placed her maternal grandmother's sapphire brooch just at her cleavage. Then she donned black satin elbow-length gloves and black satin sandals, picked up a matching evening bag, threw her sable capelet on her arm and headed for her living room. She reached it just as the bell rang.

The man who stood at her door nearly

took her breath away. He looked good enough to eat in his black tuxedo and tucked white silk shirt. They smiled at each other. She opened the door, and he entered slowly, as if at war with himself. He looked at her for a minute, smiled, took her in his arms and hugged her but didn't kiss her.

"Stunning hardly describes what I . . . what I see right now."

It amazed her that this man who always seemed in command now groped for words. Then she realized that the evening was as overwhelming for him as it was for her.

"Perhaps I'd better bring my Colt .45 along," she said to lighten the mood.

"Whatever on earth for?"

"I want to be sure that you bring me home tonight and not some other woman. And I'm serving notice that, like my forebears before me, I'm fully capable of protecting my interests."

He was perplexed for a second and then gave that rare full-throated laugh that she enjoyed so much.

As the car pulled away from the curb, Jon pressed the lever that revealed the bar, opened a bottle of champagne and filled two crystal champagne glasses. He handed one to Haley.

"To a really lovely woman," he said.

"Thank you," she said and sipped her drink.

"Nels wouldn't tell me what your background is," he said, looking intently at her. "He just said that it is very intriguing. I've done some guessing, but I want you to tell me."

"I'm twenty-eight. My father was African American from North Carolina, and my mother is Native American. Our tribe is Comanche, and most of our people are out in Oklahoma, though they are not on reservations. My parents lived and worked in Washington, DC, where my mother still lives. We lost my father twelve years ago."

"How'd your parents get to Washington, DC?"

"They both went to college there, so that's where they settled."

He nodded very slowly. "I see. Were you happy growing up?"

"Yes. We had love to spare. I have one brother who's a few years my senior. I've known two of my grandparents. My paternal grandfather used to visit us often when I was little, and he always spoke about our heritage. He was such a wonderful man, and he loved my brother and me so much that we used to say he just wrapped us up in love as if it were a blanket. I'll miss him as long as I live." He refilled their glasses.

"Are you like your mother?"

"Well, I look a bit like her, but I have my father's disposition, more or less. Why?"

"Oh, I just want to know as much as possible about you." He took her hand, stroking it gently. Without realizing it, she moved closer to him, feeling a comfort, a peace that she didn't think their relationship warranted. She sighed.

"What is it?" he asked.

How could she tell him that the night was taking on an aura of magic, that she was happy being with him? She hoped she wasn't really falling for him. After all, he was leaving, and he could meet someone and get married in the six months that he was planning to stay in Oslo — someone who spoke his native language, with whom he could read poetry and who would understand the jokes and heritage. Suddenly, her feeling of contentment was gone, and she shivered slightly.

"Are you cold?" He knew that she wasn't cold. He also knew that the feeling of togetherness that he'd felt with her just moments before had disappeared. She seemed to be slipping away from him.

He tugged gently at her arm when what he really wanted to do was clasp her tightly

68

to him and warm her from head to foot.

"Are you cold?" he repeated.

"Not really," she said, but he was not satisfied.

"Haley, I'm leaving tomorrow. I want this night with you to be special. It has to last me for six long months. And I want you to be so happy with me tonight that you'll think only of me while I'm gone."

"It is special, Jon."

Just then, the limousine came to a halt. When he assisted her from the car, she realized that they were at the Trade Winds, one of the city's finest restaurants. The maître d' greeted Jon warmly and led them immediately to their secluded table. They were seated near a waterfall, at the bottom of which grew white and purple water lilies bathed in a soft spotlight that caused the cascading water to shimmer with all the colors of the rainbow. Their table was set with white linen, long tapered candles, crystal stemware and fine silver. And at the center was a vase of white and amber orchids that Jon had ordered. The maître d' lit the candles and poured champagne.

"I can't tell you how wonderful this is, Jon. I've never felt so . . . I don't know . . . well the only word that seems right is precious."

He grinned. That was exactly the way he wanted her to feel.

"I don't expect you to believe it, but you are precious to me." When she cast her eyes downward and wouldn't look at him, he knew that his words had affected her.

He looked at Haley over the soft candlelight and felt his heartbeat accelerate. She had a powerful attraction for him. What was it that drew him to her so strongly? Since the debacle that was his marriage, he'd thought that what he had needed was a woman with passion. Now he realized that he needed and wanted more. What he wouldn't give for a woman who was a warm, loving companion. Haley gave him warmth, sweetness *and* passion the two times that he'd kissed her. Yet, she seemed to prefer distance between herself and other people, and that gave him a feeling of disquiet. He cared for her, but he did not know her. Was he risking too much? he wondered.

"Have you ever wanted to marry?" he asked her, not certain where that thought had come from.

Surprised, she hesitated. "Once, for a very brief time, I thought I did. It isn't a period of my life that I remember with pleasure or pride." Surely not, he thought, observing the sudden sadness in her eyes.

"Then we won't talk about it now," he said, in an attempt to reassure her and put her at ease again. So she'd had some bleak times, too. He wondered about the man, how he had hurt her and whether she was over him. He had to know. "Do you still care for him?"

"No, I haven't for a very long time. Perhaps I never did. I don't know, but as I look back, what I felt then seems trivial compared to . . ."

"Compared to what?"

She took the coward's course. "Compared to what I think a woman can feel . . . well, you know . . ."

He smiled inwardly. The normally poised Dr. Feldon was suddenly flustered. He didn't try to subdue the hope that rose within him.

The waiter brought them small cups of soup. Haley smiled in anticipation of the feast and lifted the round lipped silver spoon to her mouth.

"Well, well, if it isn't the goddess. Remember me?" Haley stared at the man, trying to place him.

"No, I don't remember having made your acquaintance."

"Course you do, Nels Andersen introduced us at his party."

"You don't know this man?" Jon said through clenched teeth, rising from his seat. She shook her head, and he signaled for the maître d'.

"Is there something wrong, Mr. Ecklund?" the maître d' queried nervously as he sensed hostility between the two men.

"Mario, would you show this man to a table of his own." Mario casually wiped his chin with a white handkerchief, and a big tuxedo-groomed bouncer appeared immediately and escorted Art Chasen gently but firmly to the side door.

"My apologies, Mr. Ecklund. I'm terribly sorry."

"No problem, Mario. Thanks for your assistance," Jon said as he returned to his seat.

Both the force of Jon's anger and his ability to control it told Haley much about him. He was his own man, and he could depend on his ability to control his behavior and his words. Was he controlling what he felt for her? Her upward glance confirmed her suspicions. Oh, he felt something, all right. His smoldering green eyes told her that, and they had told her before, but he wasn't ready to confirm it.

"I'm sorry about Chasen's rudeness. I met him at Nels's party and didn't like him then.

72

I like him even less now."

"Don't give it another thought."

Wanting to restore their earlier companionable mood, she grasped his left hand lightly and stroked his strong tapered fingers. He covered her hand with his right one and smiled at her. She looked at the smile that played around his sensuous lips and thought that she could happily look at him forever.

As they ate, they talked of their work, something that they hadn't done before. They discovered they shared many interests.

"Do you like working so closely with your father?"

"We're a team and a good one," he said. "I have enormous respect for his judgment and for him as a man. Yeah, I like working with him." His next thought astonished him.

"What is it?" Haley wanted to know, evidently having witnessed the abrupt change in him.

"I was thinking how much my father would like you. I think my mom would, too, but Dad would adore you. You're exactly his type of woman — intelligent, feminine, one who doesn't depend upon a man for her identity. Yes, he'll like you, no doubt about it."

"Did he like your ex-wife?" Why had she

asked that? "I'm sorry, I didn't mean to pry."

"You aren't prying. And no, he was not fond of Karen, though he was always gracious to her. Neither of my parents was happy with my marriage."

"Hmm, I've eaten so much, but this lemon-rum soufflé is wonderful."

He knew that she was changing the subject to a potentially less explosive one.

"This has really been the most delicious meal. I don't think I've ever enjoyed one more," she said and then leaned forward. "Perhaps the company is the ingredient that has made it so perfect."

"Does that mean that I get a good-night kiss?"

She half smiled. "One never plans these things. Who knows, maybe if you stay on your best behavior . . ."

"I'm always on my best behavior."

"Heaven forbid." She blushed, realizing that she'd said it aloud. "Does that mean I'll never get to see the real you?"

"Let me assure you that there's nothing saintly about me. I swim *au naturel* and sleep in the buff," he said. From the heat in her face, he knew she was imagining how he'd look emerging from a Norwegian lake dripping wet.

The waiter saved her. "Your espresso, madam, sir."

"Thanks," Haley murmured, but he could see that she was distracted.

As they made their way out of the restaurant, he walked slightly behind her with his right hand splayed at her lower back. He couldn't help but notice the way men openly appraised her as they walked to the limousine. He wasn't the only one who found her desirable. It occurred to him that six months was a long time with that kind of competition. What the hell, he thought, if she couldn't sustain an interest in him for six months just because he wasn't around, then he wouldn't have lost anything.

The limousine drove several blocks and stopped. She looked inquiringly at him but asked nothing. She was placing herself in his care this night for whatever magic he decided to spin for them. Did she trust him so much? She didn't dare question herself just now. She cast her doubts aside and took his arm when he offered it. The determined smile that she gave him belied her uncertainty. She forced herself to think of the six months when he would be away, when she would either forget about him or be undone with longing for him. At The Razor's Edge, a doorman opened the front passenger's door of the limousine. "Welcome madam, sir."

It took a lot to overwhelm Haley, but the pains that Jon had taken to make their evening memorable nearly accomplished that. Surely, she thought, he wouldn't do this for just any date. Maybe he would be different from Josh and other men she'd dated, but she wasn't going to hope for it.

The maître d' led them to their reserved table, and when the waiter brought their champagne, Jon gave him a note. Almost immediately, the orchestra played "If I Loved You." Smiling, he lifted his glass, and they silently drank to each other. Then, he stood and held out his hand to her. His nerves rattled, and his heart raced for he sensed that they were reaching a milestone in their relationship.

Haley didn't understand why she was suddenly so sharply attuned to Jon's feelings. All at once, she knew with certainty that he was as unsure about their relationship as she was. He was seeking sustenance just as she was. Like her, he was reluctant to reach out for it. So, when he opened his arms to her there on the dance floor, she let go and stepped into him. She wasn't thinking of herself, only of him. She just knew that she wanted to heal him. She put her head to his chest, her arms around his shoulders, and as she had not done before, she simply surrendered to him. She made no demands, just relaxed into him, telling him without words to take what he needed from her in that moment.

He had not previously had that experience, for most women saw him as Mr. Money Bags. So when he realized what she was telling him, his heart pounded. It wasn't passion that overcame him but joy. Pure joy. She was there for him, and she was telling him so. Her total surrender told him that she wanted to share whatever he was experiencing without question and without judging him in any way.

He lowered his head and gently kissed her eye. "Haley, you're sending me messages that give me the hope I've never had. I care for you. Feeling you in my arms like this is more than I dreamed of, ever. Don't say anything. Just . . . just be close to me, like now."

She'd been close to him before. Her kisses had electrified him, but until now, she hadn't given him herself, her compassion, her tenderness. He didn't dance with her again, just sat there with her, holding her hand and telling her his plans for the next six months. He didn't dare dance with her again in the presence of a single soul.

Their ride back to Haley's apartment was quiet and unexpectedly filled with tension. The driver waited while Jon walked Haley to her door. *So he isn't planning a big seduction scene,* she thought. She wasn't sure whether she was grateful or disappointed. He took her key and unlocked the door. She moved inward, but he didn't follow her.

"I don't suppose it makes sense to invite you in for a drink when we've just had one."

"I don't want a drink, Haley." His voice was low, husky and lacking its usual resonance.

"Then, I suppose it's good night. I had a wonderful evening with you, Jon, one that I won't soon forget. I hope you have a pleas—"

He interrupted her. "What I want right now, Haley, is you." She gasped. "But I can't have what I want," he went on. "I'm thirty-four years old and long past the point in my life where I could have a casual relationship with a woman that I care for, and I care for you. I told you yesterday that I have things to work out. I won't try to take our relationship any further until I've done that. I know that I'm asking for a lot of trust, but I'm still asking it. Perhaps during these months, you will release some of the anxieties that you have. This isn't easy for me. In fact, leaving you like this may be one of the most difficult things I have ever done."

"And six months is all you need?"

"Perhaps less, I don't know. I want us to keep in close touch. I can't tell you what I'm feeling just now. The entire evening has given me a glimpse of what a woman can be to a man . . . of what you and I could have and more. Be here for me, Haley. I told you that when I come back I want to come back to you. Don't forget that."

For a long minute, she looked at him without speaking. She knew that she wasn't ready for an affair, that she was frightened of the possibility of what one implied. He sensed her mood.

"This isn't a time for mistrust or misgivings, but for understanding and faith." As the burning intensity of his passion-filled gaze warmed her, she relaxed.

"I'll miss you, too, and I'm just having difficulty dealing with the strength of what's happening between us. We've only known each other for six weeks."

He stroked her cheek. "Sweetheart, have

you forgotten that we saw each other for months before we actually met? I was attracted to you the first time I saw you."

He opened his arms. "Come here to me." She stepped into his arms, knowing that she was probably courting despair but unwilling to forego this last opportunity to hold him and to feel herself enclosed in his masculine warmth. She lifted her arms to his shoulders and raised her parted lips for his kiss. He shuddered as her move unleashed his desire and stepped back in an effort to gain some control. But she gave no quarter, pressing into him with her softness, going after what she wanted — to merge into him and forget herself and everything but the feel of him.

"Haley, oh, Haley." He caressed her face softly, almost reverently and gazed into her eyes, as if willing her to understand what he could not say.

Frustrated with longing, she solved the problem for him, rising on tiptoe and pulling his head down to her level. She sought and found his warm sensuous lips, and he capitulated and took her to him, mutely proclaiming to her that he longed for and needed her. Wordlessly, she asked for his tongue, and when he gave it to her, she sucked on it as if it were the essence of life itself. Jon cupped her buttocks and fitted her to him. He was not accustomed to feeling a woman's need as he did then, and he knew that he was nearing his limit. He felt her full breasts pressing against him and, heedlessly, reached into her strapless gown, took her breast into his mouth and nourished himself. When he felt her shiver, he knew that he had to stop.

"Jon, if you're going to leave me, go."

He held her close for a few minutes. "Just tell me you'll be here for me. Tell me that what you've given me here tonight is real and that you'll help me work things out for us." He knew she didn't understand what he meant, yet she did not hesitate.

"I'll be here for you when you come back. I promise."

CHAPTER 3

When Jon's plane touched down at Gardermoen International Airport in Oslo, he said a prayer of thanks, as he always did. Like so many Norwegians, his folks were God fearing and had raised him to be the same. He lived by the principles that he'd been taught as a child. He tried to be as honest and truthful, and though business relations didn't always permit total honesty, he made it a rule never to compromise his honor.

He lifted his luggage from the conveyer belt and headed for customs, and his face lit up when he saw Svend waiting for him. They greeted each other warmly. Jon was the older of the two brothers by three years. He knew that Svend idolized him and had been deeply saddened when Jon's marriage ended. They had always been close, and what was pain for one was pain for the other.

"Well, kid, have you been doing anything that you can tell me about?" Jon asked

Svend in their native tongue.

"I ought to ask you that. You look as if you either won a pile of money or found a good woman. Which is it?" Noticing Jon's uncharacteristically diffident manner, Svend laughed. "Well, hell, man, tell me about her." He put his brother's bags in the trunk of his fire engine–red sports sedan, opened the passenger door for Jon, got in and headed for home.

"You've got me there, little brother. I hardly believe it myself. But there's really nothing to tell. We're just getting started. We haven't rounded any bends or passed any major milestones yet."

"But I can see that she pleases you. Can't you tell me what she's like? You know, is she over or under fifty, got all her teeth and things like that?"

"Don't be a smart-ass," Jon said, smiling.

"The important thing is whether she's got the music that makes you dance." As if sensing Jon's unspoken plea for privacy about the woman, Svend relented and changed the subject.

"Mom and Dad were surprised, better say shocked, about your sudden decision to come home for six months. Are you all right?"

"Yeah, I'm fine. I left DuPree in charge in

New York, and I've got MacKenlin covering the East Africa branch. Everything else goes on as usual. I just need some time to get my personal life together."

"There hasn't been anyone at all since Karen?"

"Until now, no one. This is important to me, Svend, but I can't talk about it just now. I'll just say that you, Mom and Dad would like her a helluva lot. She's a fine human being, not to mention a beautiful one. I don't want to raise anybody's hopes with this, including my own. So let's go easy, will you? I don't plan to say much to the folks about it. Okay?"

"Gotcha." But he could see that Svend was puzzled. He normally shared most everything with his brother; certainly he would ordinarily tell him about Haley, because she meant a great deal to him.

"Here we are. The place hasn't changed a bit." Jon looked at the pleasant white stucco two story house with its red shutters embracing high windows, its great red chimneys, inviting porches and its beautiful gardens with their wonderful spruce trees. The place was like his mother, forever nurturing him and always opening its arms to him when he returned. He loved it.

Erik and Inger Ecklund stepped out on

the porch as the car drove up. Simultaneously, they opened their arms to Jon with the welcome that they always gave their sons when one was returning home. Jon hugged them, assured them that he was fine in all respects and that there was nothing for them to worry about, though he wasn't so sure about the latter. Who knew what problems he may be starting — or even accelerating — for that matter? Well, it was something he should have done years ago. His family had always supported him. Why shouldn't they do it now?

As he began unpacking in his old room, he thought about his parents. They were still young. His father was only twenty-two years older and his mother twenty-one years older than he. He knew that they were still lovers. They adored each other, and there was clearly a strong physical attraction between them. He was happy for them, and he wanted the same for himself. He had thought he would find such a relationship with Karen, but she hadn't loved him. He had often wondered why she married him. Oh, she had pretended to be enamored of him, to be crazy about him until they married. Then he very soon realized that she had little patience with him in bed or out. It still hurt him when he remembered that she never once attempted to adjust to his needs. She would have emasculated a weaker man. Because he had sworn never to take another woman so long as he was married, he'd asked her to decide whether she would be his wife in truth or whether they should separate. She had asked for a divorce. A year later, she remarried.

Jon desperately hoped that his judgment would be better this time around. He sensed that loving Haley would be different. He wanted the love, the caring and most of all the passion his parents shared. He hoped to have that kind of relationship with Haley. Come what may, he wouldn't turn back now. He had too much to gain.

Haley replaced the phone in its cradle, walked out to Amy's desk and gave a sharp whistle. It was so uncharacteristic a gesture that Amy was speechless. "We got it! We got it!"

"We got what?" a startled Amy wanted to know.

"Brayton-Rogers came through with a million and a half. I've got to call my mother and thank her for all the help she gave us."

When Gale didn't answer her call, Haley

suddenly lost steam.

"What's the matter?" Amy asked.

"I don't know," Haley said. "I wanted this so badly. Now that I have it, something's missing."

"Call up Jon Ecklund and tell him about it, and you'll find out what's missing."

"You're way off base. Anyway, he hasn't said 'pig' to me since he left here two weeks tomorrow."

"I've always found that it's best not to lie to myself," Amy said. "That way, I'm better prepared for whatever comes, be it welcome or not."

"Thanks, Aristotle," Haley retorted, "but would you please try to reach my mother, again." She went back to her office and closed the door. Why hadn't he called or written? He'd said he wanted them to be in close touch. All right, she'd try to have patience. It was just that she hadn't expected to feel the emptiness, the awful void. She hadn't even gotten used to him, yet she missed him almost as much as if they'd been close for years. Amy interrupted her musings.

"Your mother's on the line."

"Thanks, Amy. Would you close the door, please."

"Hello, darling, what's up?"

"Oh, Mama, I got the Brayton-Rogers grant. Isn't it wonderful? I'm in the big time, a full-fledged multimillion dollar foundation. They doubled the amount that I asked for. Now, I can get to work on the East Africa program and the reservations project. You helped me tremendously, and I'm calling to thank you."

"You don't have to thank me. I'm always here for you, darling. That's what unconditional love is all about. Now when do we get together to celebrate? Why not come down for the weekend?"

Haley grabbed at the suggestion like a drowning person reaching for a rope. She hadn't known that she needed to crawl into the safety of her mother's warmth and wisdom. She didn't ask herself why she needed shelter, but she knew that she did. And in that moment she began to suspect that she might be in love with Jon Ecklund.

"I'll get the five o'clock shuttle Friday," she told her mother. "That should put me home by six forty-five." She still referred to her mother's house as home when she was speaking to her mother. "Don't meet me, the traffic will be too heavy. I'll take a taxi." She remained deep in thought for some time after she rang off. When had she fallen in love with Jon?

■ ■ ■ ■

The taxi pulled into Spring Road and stopped at her mother's home. She paid and thanked him and walked up the winding path to the red brick Tudor that was home for so many years. They greeted each other warmly. Gale was tall, less than an inch shorter than Haley and, except for their eyes, they looked much alike. Haley's eyes were light brown, Gale's were dark brown. As elegant as her daughter, she was a beautiful woman. But unlike her daughter, Gale Feldon had known the love of a man. Jack Feldon had loved her with passion for every day of the twenty-two years of their marriage. She was a woman completely fulfilled. In the end, he had a difficult illness, but he had taken great pains to prepare her for death. She would miss him all of her life, but he hadn't left her empty.

Gale looked at her daughter. "You haven't been sleeping, Hessy? Surely you weren't so concerned about the Brayton-Rogers grant that you couldn't sleep. What happened to my cool, self-confident and optimistic girl?"

Haley forced a smile. "Let me get in the door before you start interrogating me. I'm fine." She hugged her mother. "And you look great, Mama." She looked around, missing the familiarity of the furnishings that made her call the house, home. "You didn't tell me that you'd redecorated the foyer and living room." Her evasiveness did not escape Gale.

"Your brother took pains to instruct me as to the difference between antique and just plain old. He was as subtle as ever."

"How is Sky? I haven't spoken with him in a couple of weeks. I've just let everything go."

"Not everything."

Haley managed a lame smile. She would never get around Gale's sharp eyes, and for the first time in her adult life, she wanted to see her mother as a friend. She wanted open honesty that she had never permitted herself with anyone. The thought occurred to her that she didn't have one close friend. Amy tried to be a friend, but she had erected a barrier, never letting Amy get too close. In the Peace Corps, she'd been buddies with all of her colleagues but friends with none of them. She'd never given it a thought — never needed to. Now, in a moment of candid self-appraisal, she saw that her tranquil, successful life was, in fact, a very lonely one. She couldn't know that the look she gave her mother was one of despair.

"Go up and put your things away, dear. I thought we'd have dinner at home tonight, give us both a chance to unwind."

"Okay, be right back." Haley changed into a yellow jogging suit, which she only wore at home, as she never jogged. She walked slowly down the stairs, thinking how comforting it was to be with Gale. She had a mother who didn't criticize her, didn't lecture to her and didn't try to run her life. Yet she knew that her mother loved her fiercely.

They watched the news on the cable channel while they sipped white wine and nibbled cheese straws. Gale served a simple dinner, and after they finished eating and cleaned, Gale took Haley by the hand and led her into the den.

"Hessy, I don't intend to pry, but I can see that you are troubled, and I want to know what I can do to help." To Haley's surprise and horror, she began to cry, and within seconds, she was sobbing uncontrollably. Gale held her for a few minutes until the sobbing subsided.

"Does he love you?"

"What? What did you say?"

"Does he love you?"

"Oh, Mama. Why do you think it's a man?"

"Because I know my daughter, and you're in love. I was beginning to wonder if it would ever happen."

"Well, there was Josh."

"Bull, you didn't love Josh. Why are you crying for this man?"

"I miss him so much. I didn't realize that I love him until he went home. Mama, why would a man who says he cares for a woman leave her for six months without making any effort to take her to bed? He says that there's no other woman in his life."

"I suppose he had a reason, though I can't imagine what it would be. Why don't you start at the beginning?" Gale waited until Haley finished her story before she spoke. "Why can't you trust him? There's no such thing as love without trust."

"I'm trying. I'm really trying." If she hadn't been upset and had been her usually perceptive self, Haley would have been aware of her mother's look of pure satisfaction.

"I can understand why you're concerned that you haven't heard from him, though you didn't give him any reason to believe that you'd be waiting with bated breath. But, Hessy, nothing you've told me explains why you're so unhappy."

"I know. I don't know how to say this. I —"

Gale interrupted her. "Just say it. I'm not your judge. I'm your mother, and I love you no matter what you do."

"Mama, if Jon had asked me to make love with him, I don't know what I would have done. I don't think I could face the devastating humiliation that —"

Gale sprang to her feet, interrupting her daughter. "Why would a twenty-eight-year-old woman think that she would be devastated if she shared her body with a man who cares for her and whom she loves, a man with whom she shares a powerful attraction? That man you described to me would cherish a woman. What happened between you and Josh?"

"Oh, Mama, he hurt me. And when I couldn't respond the way he wanted, he said terrible things. Please don't ask me to repeat them."

"I see. He didn't bring you to climax?"

"No. I mean, I don't even know what that is."

"Good Lord! And he's the only one?"

"What's worse maybe is that sometimes when I'm with Jon I remember how cruel Josh was to me that night and how he humiliated me. Jon looks white, but he isn't really —"

"Wait a minute. You're not suggesting that every white man would be like Josh, for heaven's sake."

"No, I'm not, Mama, but I think about how Daddy treated you and how gentle he was, and from my childhood, I dreamed of marrying a man like him. Maybe I should stick close to my roots."

Gale ran her fingers through her long silky hair, punishing her scalp. "What do you mean? He's Norwegian, but he's not white?"

"His mother is African American. She married his father and went to live in Norway. I gather that, except for his curly hair, which is blond, he looks like his father."

Gale released a long sigh. "We're off the subject. I forget how good you are at that. Are you telling me that there hasn't been a man in your life since Josh?"

"There's been no one else. Maybe he acted as he did because his folks didn't approve of me. I don't know, and I'm not sure I have the guts to go that way again." She walked to the window, looked out at the moonlit garden and felt her mother's gentle hand on her shoulder.

"That had nothing to do with him as a man. Josh cheated you. He was inadequate, perhaps just inexperienced, and he knew it, but he led you to believe that the problem lay with you. He did a cruel thing. In the first place, he should have been gentle with you. Then, if he didn't satisfy you with his God-given male equipment, he has two hands, a mouth and a tongue, and he should have used them. Damn! Nothing's more distressing than a man who's ignorant, selfish or both. Promise me that when you and Jon reach the point of intimacy that you'll tell him about this, including the part that you didn't tell me."

"Mama, I couldn't do that."

"If you don't tell him, how will he repair the damage? And believe me, he will repair it. I'm putting my money on him. The person that you described to me is a real man."

"You've never shown me this side of you before, Mama. I mean, I never saw you as being, well, you know, such a woman. I don't know exactly how to phrase it, but you know what I mean."

"Honey, I know what a man and a woman can be to each other. I had the love of a man who adored me, and I want that for my daughter. Your father gave himself to me completely because I let him. I welcomed him. He knew that I wanted him anytime and all of the time. He didn't have to lay a big scene for me, just open his arms and let me know that he needed me." She struggled to control the tears, but they came anyway.

She went on. "You can't have what love promises with your man if you don't open up to him, if you don't share your thoughts, dreams, fears, sorrows and joys with him. You can't have it if you're looking only for your own pleasure, for what you can get. A man and a woman have to be there for each other in the most selfless way. And, darling, if you're there for him when he needs you, when you're in his arms, your man will take you to heaven with him."

Gale sat quietly for a while, and Haley was so struck by what she knew had been a personal account by her mother that she was without words. Finally, Gale spoke. "I haven't remarried, because I know that I can't duplicate your father. And even if I could find such a man, I wouldn't break my vows to Jack Feldon. I'll love him even after I'm dead."

Haley had lost interest in celebrating her success at fundraising. So when Gale raised her glass in toast a few minutes later, she stopped her mother.

"I'd rather just remember right now the love that I've known from the time that I was conceived. I've never thought much lately about you and Daddy, but I know that you loved each other deeply and that Sky and I were lucky to have you two as parents. If I'm fortunate enough with a man I love to have just half of what you had, I'll be satisfied."

"It isn't all luck, my dear. I try to restrict my lectures to the classroom, but I can't resist telling you that your professional accomplishments shouldn't be the only important thing in your life, certainly not the most important. Which would have hurt you most, losing Jon or losing the Brayton-Rogers grant?"

"I don't have Jon, yet, Mama, and a lot of things have to be resolved between us before we get any closer."

Gale regarded her sadly. "Pain is a great teacher, and loneliness can conquer pride and fear. I'm looking forward to meeting the man who has cracked my daughter's carefully constructed veneer."

When Haley walked into her apartment Sunday afternoon, she saw the light on her answering machine. She got a glass of lemonade, kicked off her shoes and sat down to check her calls. Nels wanted to have lunch with her on Monday, the neighborhood florist asked for a return call and then she heard his voice, "Haley, I've tried to reach you four times this weekend, and I've finally decided to leave a message. I hate to talk into these things. Call me, would you? I miss you. Jon."

She laughed aloud, partly from pent-up emotion and the anxiety she'd been experiencing at not having heard from him and partly from his assumption that she wouldn't recognize his voice. She punched in his phone number, noting from her watch that it was already eleven o'clock in Oslo. It shocked her to realize that she had memorized the number, though she'd only looked at it once when he gave her his card the last night they were together.

"Hello." She felt the tremors from her head to her toes. Suddenly, she found herself lying flat on her back on the sofa, hugging herself.

"I'm sorry I missed your calls, Jon. I was in Washington spending the weekend with Mama." How could her voice be so calm when she felt like a volcano inside?

"Did you get my flowers?"

"No, but I got a message from my florist that I should let her know when I got home. Thank you. However, my first act was to call you. I'm sorry that I'm calling so late, but it's only five o'clock in the afternoon here."

"I wouldn't care if it was five o'clock in the morning. I wanted to hear your voice, and anyway, I'm not sleeping."

"You could have heard me sooner, if you'd called."

"Touché! Actually, I haven't been here. As soon as I arrived, I found that I had to look into some problems in our Southeast Asia branch, and I left the next day for Bangkok. I found such a mess there that I was at it sometimes eighteen to twenty hours a day. I got back yesterday. I just want to know one thing. Have you missed me?"

"I've missed you, and this is going to be a long six months." She gambled, hoping that he would give her something more than that he'd missed her, but knowing in her heart that he wouldn't, couldn't until he'd worked through whatever problem he had.

"Yeah, it is that," was his cryptic response.

"Thank you again for the flowers, Jon. I'm sure it's time you slept. We'll talk again, good night." There was another long silence before he said good-night. She sat up on the sofa, feeling bereft and forlorn.

Jon pulled his pillow under his right arm and covered it with his left. What had he wanted to say to her? When he'd called, there'd been so much he'd wanted to tell, to share. The personnel problems in Southeast Asia were threatening the company's very existence. For once, he and his father did not agree on a solution. Now his father had gone to see what he could do to settle staff agitations and especially the problem with reporting and who knew when he would return.

There had been no opportunity for him to speak with his father about his personal concerns. So his life was still on hold. He knew that their telephone conversation had disappointed Haley, as it had him, but he didn't know how to amend it. His feelings for her went even deeper than he had thought when he left. But he didn't really know how she felt about him. He knew that she was attracted to him and that she responded to him. She seemed to care about him. So why had he left her hanging at the end of that call?

He went downstairs to the library, helped himself to some scotch and went back to bed. An hour later, unable to sleep he called her. When she answered, he wasted no time.

"Haley, what I really called you for was to tell you that I need you. I'm lonely for you, and I've got all kinds of professional concerns that I want to share with you and no one else. I need to be with you, and having to talk with you this way was so frustrating. Forgive me for having been so uncommunicative."

"There was so much that I wanted to say, too. I'm glad you called back. There are things that I've wanted to share with you, too. For instance, when I learned that Brayton-Rogers had not only agreed to provide the grant that I was requesting but had doubled it I was unhappy because I couldn't tell you."

"That's great news. Does that mean that having dinner with me really did solve the problems you were having with it?" She laughed that low throaty laugh that he liked so much.

"Hardly! Well, there may have been a relationship. The next day, I got down to business and got the job done. Of course, I might have done that anyway," she joked.

"I won't push it." Feeling uplifted and knowing exactly why, he savored the silence for a moment and then, in a lowered, husky voice that betrayed his true feelings he spoke, "I'll call you again soon. Good night, sweetheart. Dream about me." He hung up before she could respond. He slept soundly the rest of the night.

■ ■ ■ ■

Haley was less fortunate than Jon. She lay in the dark thinking about the calls, what he hadn't said the first time and all that he'd said during the second call. He'd said that he needed and missed her, called her his sweetheart and asked her to dream about him.

She'd been in bed for hours and couldn't get to sleep for thinking of him and how much she wanted to be with him. After counting sheep and saying the multiplication tables backward till dawn, she took a sleeping pill and sent a text message to Amy saying that she would be in in the afternoon. Finally, she drifted off to sleep.

Jon had become impatient. It had been two weeks since his father went to Bangkok, and he gave no indication that his return home was imminent. His dad hadn't been out in the field for a while and probably wanted to touch base with as many regional bureaus as possible. Jon rejoiced that his father retained an active interest in EIS, but the timing was unfortunate. He couldn't wait much longer to know whether he was doomed to the life he'd lived for the past five years. He always found it difficult to speak candidly about highly personal matters. And though his father was close to both his sons, he made it a point never to invade their privacy. Perhaps he should discuss the matter with his father only as a last resort. He wouldn't speak to Svend, because he suspected that his brother didn't have the problem. That left his mother. She might have the answers he needed.

He got out of bed, dressed casually in jeans and a red plaid cotton shirt and walked down to the kitchen where he knew he'd find his mother. It was Saturday morning, and Svend, who was spending the weekend at his parents' home, had already gone to the gym. Inger Ecklund looked up at her elder son, smiled warmly and poured him a cup of coffee. "Morning, Mom. You always spoil me. I could have done that. Just sit with me while I drink it. You want one?"

"No, thanks. I had two cups with Svend. I don't think I should have any more."

"Your health's all right, isn't it?"

"Oh, yes. As far as I know, I'm just fine. I've got some fresh bread, smoked salmon and eggs this morning. How about some?"

"Thanks. Every time I come home, I wonder how I'm able to stay away."

"What's bothering you, son?" Her question stunned him.

"Something's bothering me, Mom?"

"You know there is. Ever since you got home. I figured you'd say something before now."

"Well, as a matter of fact there is something, but I'm not sure whether I should discuss it with you or Dad." He watched her as she waited for his reply and knew without a doubt that no matter what he had to say she would receive it with the love and sympathy that had always set her apart from every other person in his life.

"Mom, did you ever wonder why Karen and I couldn't make it?"

"No, I didn't, because I knew that she hadn't brought you the love of a mature woman. In fact, I never thought she loved you. She liked the glamour that she thought you represented."

"You're right about that, and she quit acting as soon as we got married. The problem was that I couldn't reach her. She never showed me the understanding and, well, the feeling I needed if . . . what I'm trying to say is that I couldn't make an adjustment with her. She didn't try. I never expected the women that I dated more casually before I got married to show that kind of understanding, but I had thought that my wife would. What I had with Karen was so, well, so devastating that I swore never to be vulnerable to another woman."

"And now you are." It wasn't a question, but a statement of fact.

"Now, I am. I think I'm in love. I want her desperately, but I'm unable to open up to her. The last time we were together, she was so loving and compassionate. I was certain that she would have taken me right then if I had let what we were feeling run its natural course. But I had to back off. I couldn't risk it. That's why I put some distance between us and came home for a while. I wanted to see if you and Dad had any experience with this and perhaps get help in solving it. The problem is —"

She interrupted him, knowing that the details would be too painful for him to disclose. "I know what the problem is, son. You inherited it. And yes, it can be solved." Relief washed over him like rain over arid soil.

"But why haven't you mentioned this before? I'm so sorry that I haven't known. How you must have suffered! It can be solved, but it is not you who can solve it."

"What do you mean?"

"What you've just told me about your last meeting with your girl reminds me of my courtship with your father. I knew that he cared deeply for me and that he wanted me. But he always backed off just when I thought he'd surely tell me he loved me. I was frustrated and hurt, and I didn't know what to think because, in those days, he was not great at communicating. But I also sensed that he didn't want to give up on me. Each time we were together, his love for me seemed to be stronger. After sleepless nights and much self-doubt and fear, I gambled and told him that I wouldn't see him again, that I wanted a husband and a family and that he didn't seem to be headed in that direction. I told him that if he wanted to see me anymore he'd have to let me know what his intentions were.

"He was troubled. On the steps of my parents' back porch, I sat on his lap and asked him to tell me what was bothering him. I told him that I loved him and that no matter what he told me I would accept it sympathetically. He put his arms around me and confessed that he loved me but that he had a handicap that was vital to our relationship and that he didn't know how to share it with me.

"I didn't know what to expect, but after he told me that he loved me, I made up my mind to get him if I had to seduce him. He was silent for fifteen or twenty minutes and so was I. I just hugged him and caressed him. You might say I lulled him into telling me. The next day I went to the doctor and asked her how I could make love with a man who was especially large. She assured me that all I needed was love, patience and tenderness. I had plenty of all three.

"That same evening, I went to your father's apartment, uninvited and unannounced, and I seduced him. I shall never forget the moment when finally he was in my arms and we were at last as close as we could get from head to toe. He wept at his release. I have never been so happy before or since. And to this day, every time I look at you, I just overflow with love for you. It was at that moment that you were conceived."

Jon sat riveted in the spot, stunned. He hadn't expected that either of his parents would be so forthcoming. He rounded the table, took his mother in his arms and hugged her.

"Now I know why my father loves you so deeply and cherishes you so."

"Jon, do you think I didn't love him more for the faith he showed in me when he let me see his terrible vulnerability and because he allowed me to give him something so precious? Love is giving, not only receiving. Tell me something about your girl. Most important, does she love you?"

"I'll tell you what I can. I know that she cares for me," he said.

"Have you told her that you love her?"

"No. But I've told her that I think I'm falling in love with her. That was as much as I felt I could say at the time."

"Take your time with her, Jon, and teach her to love you. I think, from what you've told me, that Haley is a strong woman but that she needs assurance of her womanhood. You can give her that. Talk to her. Share this burden with her. If you don't let her know that you trust her enough to show her your vulnerability, how will you know that she's the woman for you? And don't forget, it's one thing to tell her that you need her and something else to show her. From what you've said, I'd say she cares a great deal for you. I want to meet her."

He considered all that his mother told him. She had made it clear to him that he had to do what he'd sworn never to do again and that he had to do it on blind faith. In other words, he could either risk it or walk away.

He looked at the gold watch that his parents gave him when he graduated from college and saw that he'd been sitting there for over three hours. He glanced up at the clear blue sky and around him at the still trees that were fast losing their summer elegance and wondered what his life would be like a year from then. Some inner voice told him very plainly that nothing would change unless he had the courage to set that change in motion. He had sat in that spot against that same tree hundreds of times, since he had been barely old enough to walk. Now he looked at the rushing waters below him and thought, for the first time and much to his surprise, that not even a dam could reverse the river's flow. With that, he stood up and headed back to the house. He'd made a decision, and he wouldn't reverse it.

Around that time, Haley, too, came to a decision — one that had been long coming and that would one day have an important effect on her life. She punched the intercom button, "Amy, would you please ask Spencer to come to my office."

Fully ten minutes later, the sullen man sauntered into her office. She had long suspected that he didn't like having a woman as boss, but that being the case, he should have found another job. "You sent for me?"

"Yes. Clean out your desk. This is your last day. I'm tired of your attitude. Amy will give you your severance check. That's all."

"What the hell? You can't —"

She didn't look up. "If you need assistance leaving, I'm sure that one of the guards will be glad to provide it."

She punched the intercom. "Amy, would you please get me a list of suitable applicants for Spencer's position?"

"Yes, ma'am. With the greatest of pleasure!"

Three days later, Haley interviewed Nina Emory. "Come in, Ms. Emory."

After talking with the woman for a few minutes, she liked her, but she needed to test the woman's professional depth. Half an hour later, she was satisfied that Nina Emory would be an asset to the institute.

"When can you start? I need you now," Haley said as she stood and shook Nina's hand.

"I've already given notice that I'll leave my position as soon as I find a better-paying job, but I think I still owe my boss a week's notice."

"You certainly do. I'll expect you a week from Monday."

She decided to treat herself to a gourmet

lunch, satisfied that she had passed an important milestone, that she had the self-confidence to hire someone whose competence she thought about equal to her own.

"Mr. Andersen's on the line, Haley."

"Hello, Nels. What was that economical message on my answering machine all about? Were you saving breath?"

He chuckled. "Hi. I hate talking into those blasted machines, but I guess they do serve a purpose." Who else had said that to her within the past twenty-four hours? "How about lunch tomorrow? I'd hoped to see you today, but you're rather late making your morning calls, aren't you?"

Haley laughed. She had never been able to understand why she had always felt so much at ease with Nels. He was good looking, charismatic and very masculine, yet she had never been attracted to him physically. But she valued him as a friend. The realization that Nels knew her better than Jon did startled her. He interrupted her musings. "Are you still there, love?"

"Yes, I was thinking. Where shall we meet for lunch?"

"I'll let you choose. By the way, how long has it been since you thought of Jon?"

"Drat you, Nels," she said, unable to

control a giggle. "I don't like having my mind read."

CHAPTER 4

She settled down to the task of outlining the program for the reservations and soon found herself chewing on the end of her pencil, a habit she thought she had broken in fifth grade. She got up, walked to the window and looked down on one of the city's many parks. This one had a waterfall, lovely greenery and white wrought iron chairs, benches and tables to accommodate the office lunch crowd that preferred a brown bag and thermos to a restaurant. For a fleeting moment, she wished that she were free to spend an hour in the sun. She stared into space, seeing nothing, her thoughts on Jon and what might face them.

She couldn't imagine what demons a man could have, and she didn't see how she could expose herself, her weaknesses, and her pain to him. She hadn't even been able to tell her mother all that had hurt her. He'd think her less than a woman. How could there possibly be a future for her and Jon? And what if she started to make love with him and his face became Josh's face? The face that tormented her.

"Would you like tea, Haley?" Amy came in with two cups and a plate of ginger snaps. Startled, she quickly got herself under control but not before Amy was able to assess the situation.

"Thanks, I'd love some. Sit for a minute." It was their custom to have afternoon tea together.

"Haley, have you decided to do something about your feelings for Jon?"

"What makes you think I feel something special for him?"

"Who are you trying to kid? Since that morning when he came here to see you, I've known that he had turned you completely around. Oh, you put up a good front most of the time. But right now you're hurting. Go home and call him. Tell him how you feel."

"My dear Amy, if only it were that simple," Haley said with feeling.

Lunch with Nels the next day brought her pseudo relief. It gave her the opportunity to think and talk about Jon without feeling shame or guilt.

"Haley, whatever you do, if you want Jon, play it absolutely straight with him. He won't forgive you for less," Nels said as they parted that afternoon.

"I don't play games with men, Nels. I don't even know how." He considered that for a moment but didn't respond. He simply kissed her on the cheek and then walked away.

Days later, lighthearted after a day of reasonable accomplishment at work, Haley went home feeling good. There, discovering that she needed milk and other food items, she put on a light coat and went to the supermarket. She returned home and was searching her purse for her keys when she heard a deep masculine voice behind her.

"Want me to hold that for you?" Stunned at hearing that voice, she dropped both bags of groceries, her purse and her keys, swung around and flew into Jon's arms.

"Where'd you come from? I thought you were in Oslo. How'd you get here? Why didn't you tell me you were coming? Oh, I'm so glad to see you!"

A stunned Jon had expected a welcome but none such as this. When he could get his breath, he held her away from him for a minute and studied her. Then he crushed her to him, groaning from the sweet joy, from the all-enveloping peace he knew at that moment just for having her in his arms. He kissed her eyes, her cheeks, her forehead and her eyes again. And then, as if he had tortured himself for as long as he could bear it, he put his mouth upon hers and loved her with all the fierceness of the passion that he felt for her. When he tasted the salt of her tears, he spoke to her at last. "What is it? What's the matter, baby? Why are you crying? Have I held you too tight? I'm sorry."

"Nothing's wrong. I mean, you didn't . . . you couldn't hold me too tight. I'm so glad to see you I could scream. Why have you come back? It's only been two months, and you said —"

"I came back because I just couldn't stay away any longer. I had to see you. I have to go back, but I . . . I just needed to be with you." He looked around. "Honey, we're standing in the corridor. Don't you want to let me come in?" She laughed, a joyous sound of happiness and relief. Together, they got the door open.

"I could come home to a welcome like that every day. The only person who's ever hugged me when I walked in the door is my mother."

He shrugged, but inwardly her reaction buoyed him and raised his hopes. "I got into JFK Airport about two hours ago and came straight here. My bags are downstairs. I didn't know whether you were home." She lifted the intercom phone.

"Mike, would you please send Mr. Ecklund's bags up."

"Sure thing, Dr. Feldon. Be up in a minute."

She turned to Jon, feigning displeasure. "If you'd warned me to expect you, I wouldn't look like such a mess."

"Honey, you look better to me right now than anybody or anything I've ever seen. You're beautiful. You don't need any props. I missed you," he said.

"I know you aren't hungry, since first-class passengers are fed to death practically, but would you like a drink or something?"

"No, thanks. Actually, I don't enjoy drinking when I'm tired."

"Oh, that's right. Nels said that you don't drink much, anyway."

"You've seen Nels?"

"We had lunch together today."

"I see."

"What do you see? You don't object to my having lunch with Nels, do you? He's like a brother."

"That's a good one. Nels Andersen like a brother to a beautiful available woman."

"Yes. One with whom I spent the entire lunch talking about his best friend, Jon." The doorbell rang, and she let Mike in with Jon's bags.

"He must have changed a lot since we were schoolmates."

He took her hand, sat on the sofa and beckoned her to join him. She didn't know what to expect from him. First his sudden appearance and then, his almost nonchalant behavior. Jon Ecklund did not strike her as an impulsive man.

How should she respond to him? She wanted to be close to him, so she sat beside him and would have put an arm around him. But to her bemusement, Jon put his head in her lap and stretched out with his feet hanging over the sofa arm. Then he sighed and went to sleep.

Haley gazed down at the peaceful expression on his face. Would a man do that if he didn't care deeply for the woman? She guessed she could stop worrying about how he felt. After all, he was there with her, and he could have been many other places. No, the old Haley whispered to her, she couldn't relax her guard. Josh had done hundreds of things that convinced her of his eternal love,

118

and how had he behaved? Could she trust her judgment? What choice did she have? She loved this man, and she wanted him.

She stroked his beautiful hair and, in response, he snuggled closer to her. Her heart skipped a beat and then thudded rapidly. His absolute trust disconcerted her. It was as if he'd said, "To hell with vulnerability, she has to take me as I am." She leaned over and kissed his hair, then closed her eyes and gave thanks for the consuming peace that enveloped her.

An hour later, neither of them had moved. She feasted her eyes on him. And as she bent to kiss his cheek, he opened his eyes and looked at her. What she saw in his eyes made her shiver. The naked hunger, raw need and desperate longing shook her to the very core of her being. Forgetting her caution, she hugged him closer to her and spread kisses all over his face.

Slowly, Jon disengaged himself and sat up. He wanted her so badly. Things just couldn't continue as they were. While she'd thought he was asleep, she had been so sweet and tender with him. She hadn't resented his inattentiveness, because he was tired. Instead, she'd stroked and soothed him. He gave her a piercing look, deciding on one more gamble. "I think I'd better go on to my apartment. I'm beat. I've been up for twenty-six hours."

"You may stay here, if you'd like. I have a guest room." Her flaming face betrayed her embarrassment. She couldn't invite him to share her room and her bed. He'd never asked her for that level of intimacy.

He remained silent, trying to decide how to put her at ease.

"I know you're too tired to go across town and into an apartment that you haven't seen for over two months. So stay here," she said in a rush.

He raised one eyebrow. "And if I'm not tired?"

"Oh, honey! Let's not banter like this. What do you want to do?"

"Sweetheart, we'd better not discuss what I'd really like to do. Thank you for offering to put me up tonight. The truth is, I would very much like to stay here with you. And your guest room will be fine. Tomorrow, we'll talk."

She showed him to his room and busied herself turning back the covers, opening the windows, giving instructions about the alarm clock, the bathroom, the soap, the towels and everything that she could think of to cover the awkwardness of the situation and as an excuse not to leave him. She looked up from her newly found task of fluffing his pillow and saw his gentle, tender smile.

He walked over to her and draped his arm across her shoulder. "Sweetheart, stop fussing. I want to sleep in your bed just as much as you want me to be there, but tonight isn't right for us. Our time will come — and soon." With that, he kissed her, popped her affectionately on her bottom and pushed her out the door.

Haley wasn't certain how she got into her bed that night. Even after she lay down, she continued to tremble uncontrollably. In the past seven years, since the fiasco with Josh, she had cried twice — when she had finally told her mother about it a few weeks back and after she hung up on Jon. Now she wanted to lie in his arms so badly that she was tempted to go to him.

"You're a big girl, Haley, and you can't have everything you want when you want it," she told herself. "Give him a chance." With that thought, she curled up with the pillow tight in her arms and slept.

Jon lay in the darkness. He knew that Haley was distressed, because from time to time he heard sounds that suggested she was thrashing in bed. But he also knew that if they were to have any chance together he had to control his urge to go to her. If he went into that room, all would be lost. He was perspiring so profusely that his bedding was wet. He moved over to the other side of the double bed, but he could not find peace, either. After a while, he turned on the light and looked for something to read. When she went into his room to awaken him with a cup of coffee the next morning, she found Jon asleep with a copy of Washington Irving's *Legend of Sleepy Hollow* cradled in his arm. He awakened to her feathery kiss on his lips.

"Hi, sleepy eyes," she whispered, smiling as he lifted his lashes and gazed at her.

"I get coffee in bed? Honey, you'd better be careful, I spoil easily."

"Fear not. I'll keep score and make sure that your spoiling is properly rationed."

He savored the coffee. It was hot and strong just as he liked it, with only a touch of sugar.

"How did you know how I like my coffee?"

"I just paid attention. I'm going out so you can get dressed. Meet you in the kitchen in seven minutes."

"Why seven and not six or eight?"

"You'd have made a great lawyer."

"So they say. Okay, scat. Now I have only six minutes." The vision of her sitting on the side of his bed awakening him with a kiss made him want to sing. "Haley, you make me happy," he said as she began to leave the room.

She looked at him for a long minute, and he knew she realized that, in greeting him as she had, she'd made a statement to him, and he had read it correctly. Perhaps without consciously intending to do so, she had committed herself to him.

Haley went quickly out of the room and closed the door. Nels's words came back to her: "If you want Jon, play it absolutely straight with him." She wouldn't fold up. She was a woman, no longer the foolish, idealistic girl who had swallowed Josh's hype and lies and who had allowed herself to feel diminished because Josh's parents proved to be racists. Shrugging off worries with a jerk of her right shoulder, she walked swiftly to her room. Changed and laughing, she headed for the kitchen. Jon joined her a minute short of the ultimatum she'd given him.

"Ecklund, you didn't give me a proper good morning kiss," she said playfully.

"You've got to be kidding. If you thought I was going to kiss you in that bed after the night I had . . . have pity, woman." He grinned and kissed her on the nose. "I don't want an early death, and a few more hours like those and you can start sending out black bordered announcements. What do you usually do on Saturdays?"

"Things around the house, nothing special. Why?"

He reached across the table and stroked the back of her hand. "I came back here to see you. But I think I ought to try and spend a couple of hours at least with DuPree. He's managing the shop here." He looked at her intently. "Can you handle that?"

He hoped that her sparkling eyes reflected the happiness she felt. "Just be here properly dressed by seven o'clock this evening."

Was she really as understanding as she seemed? Jon wondered. First, last night he'd fallen sleep with his head in her lap and now this. He remembered how agreeable Karen had been before he married her. But Karen had never been as compassionate as Haley. Anyway, why the hell was he standing there looking a gift horse in the mouth? He'd promised himself that he was going to trust her.

"Why seven o'clock? Are you partial to the number seven?"

"No, I'm not partial to that number. I like to eat shortly after that, and I'm inviting you to dinner tonight."

"Are we going out?"

"I want you to know, Mr. Ecklund, that I'm a good cook. And since you're such a skeptic, come prepared for a gourmet meal."

"Tell you what," he offered. "I'll check with DuPree, and then we'll make plans."

Jon went to the room she'd given him and sat on the edge of the bed. He phoned Jason DuPree and arranged to see him at three o'clock. He called a taxi and headed for his apartment, eager to shorten the day.

Haley leaned against the door jamb of her pantry and thought of all that had happened during the past twenty-four hours, from her luncheon with Nels and his prophetic admonishments regarding Jon, to Jon's unanticipated visit, their strange evening and, most of all, what might happen that evening when he returned.

She felt herself more able to cope with the dizzying changes in her life than she had ever been. And it occurred to her that her faith and trust in Jon, her certain knowledge of his strength and of his need for her were as much responsible as her own strength.

Suddenly, she began to falter. The telephone rang and, because she didn't want anything or anyone to intrude on those precious minutes, she walked past it. But thinking that it might be Jon, she turned back and picked up the receiver.

To her relief, she heard her mother's voice. "Hessy, what's wrong? I can barely recognize your voice."

"Nothing, really. I've just got a lot on my mind just now."

"Haven't you heard from Jon?" She could always rely on her mother to get right to the point.

"Mama, Jon's here. He showed up yesterday evening saying that he had to see me."

"Where is he now?"

"Over at his apartment."

"Haley Feldon, are you crazy? Why isn't he with you?"

"It's all right, Mama. He just went to look after a few things. He'll be back. We're spending the evening together."

"I should hope so. Remember what I told you."

"I remember. Oh, Lord, I'm glad you called just now. You have an uncanny way of knowing when I need to talk to you. I had begun to doubt myself just as the phone rang, but I'll be fine now."

"He's your man. Forget everything that

has happened before with any other man. I'll be thinking about you, dear."

Humming and singing songs that she loved, Haley prepared for an evening that would change her life. To save time, she ordered groceries and flowers by phone. She set her table with fine linen, silverware, crystal and porcelain, added candles in silver candle holders to complete the centerpiece of calla lilies and tea roses. She put two bottles of wine in the refrigerator.

Maybe she was overdoing it, but she wanted to show him that he deserved the best she had to offer. Get real, she advised herself. You know that you are about to change your life, and you want to do it in style. What would he be like? How was she going to feel when he was finally inside of her?

Damn her inexperience! She wanted to be everything to him, but if she made mistakes, he would know that she was trying and that her heart was in the right place. She just prayed that that would be enough.

She had planned a meal that wouldn't require her to spend any time in the kitchen after Jon arrived. She looked at her watch and realized that she'd better hurry. After a shower, she washed her hair and sprayed her favorite scent all over her body. Then she patted herself dry, applied a body lotion of the same scent and left the steamy bathroom. As she passed the mirror, she wondered if he would like the way she looked. She knew that she had a good figure, but not every man liked a woman with a full bosom and squared shoulders. Well, she was what she was, and that was that.

She slipped on a pair of mauve-pink silk lace bikini panties and a matching bra that gave minimum support and covered nothing. It was six-thirty. She brushed her long black hair until it shone, applied pink lipstick and put on one of her favorite dinner dresses, a mauve-pink silk jersey floor-length sheath with a slit up to the middle of her left thigh. Satisfied with the results, she put on some music, Mozart for dinner and, after that, soulful love songs. The doorbell rang. She waited in front of the door for several seconds before she opened it.

"Can't I come in? Why do I always have such a heck of a time getting into your apartment?" As his facial expression melted into a smile, she reached up and kissed him lightly on the lips. "Hi. You look wonderful." She was acutely aware of him. The sight of him made her mouth water.

"You knock me out, looking like this for me alone," he teased, trying to keep it light. She knew that she seemed self-conscious avoiding his eyes and caressing her sides as though they were cold, but actually she wasn't self-conscious; she was on the verge of losing her battle with self-control. She wanted to wrap herself around him, to disappear inside of him. And she didn't know what to do about it. When she closed the door, he handed her a box of two dozen red roses. She turned to get a vase, but he pulled her to him and kissed her hungrily. Reaching behind, she laid the flowers on the table, then wrapped her arms around him and let him have his way.

"I love this color on you. Hell! I love you," he said after ending the kiss.

As she went toward the kitchen for the vase, he followed her. "I've brought some wine and a bottle of champagne," he said, putting three bottles into the refrigerator. "Where's the food? Didn't you cook? I don't smell a thing, and I don't see anything. Woman, you're dealing with a hungry man, here."

Haley laughed. She had felt so much at

ease with him this morning, but now he seemed to be in a more playful mood. She gloried in the intimacy and found it fun to tease him.

"Go back into the living room where you belong. My wonderful music is going to waste."

How he treasured the togetherness that he felt with her! "Yeah. That piece is one of my favorites. What else have you got in store for me?" He'd been jesting, carried away by the wonderful, lighthearted fun they were sharing, something that he'd rarely enjoyed. But the minute he'd said it, he wanted to eat the words. He didn't want her to be nervous with him or to feel any pressure from him. He was content to wait. To his surprise, however, she didn't take exception to the remark.

"I know I gambled in not asking what you like and dislike, but I hope you'll be pleased."

He was so grateful for the reprieve that he disowned having *any* dislikes where food was concerned. He winced. If she had prepared calves brains, he was in serious trouble. She placed the drinks on a serving cart in the living room and asked him to mix them. As they sat quietly, he sipped a vodka tonic and she a Cotton Picker cocktail. Aware only of the wonder of being together, they listened to the last movement of the concerto.

When he draped his arm lightly around her shoulder, she shifted a little closer to him. "Can you stay put while I get our dinner going? By staying put, I mean staying in here."

"I suppose I could."

She wrinkled her nose at him and left the room. He tried to assess her mood and to anticipate the evening, but he was afraid to believe what he sensed. Well, he'd take it as it came. How had she picked so many of his favorite music pieces for their time together? Not many people were likely to have a recording of Dittersdorf's bass concerto. And those Duke Ellington, Ray Charles and Mozart numbers had been his favorites since he was in college.

"Come to dinner." He loved her soft, sultry voice. God, he could listen to it forever. She met him at the door of the dining room and walked in with him. The courtesy wasn't wasted on him; he was accustomed to fine manners. It pleased her to see that her efforts impressed him. Now if only he liked the meal. He seated her and then took his own chair.

She had placed bowls of wild mushroom

soup before them. "Haley, this is wonderful. How many courses are we having? It's one of my favorite soups. If you didn't cook too big a meal, I could have some more of this."

"You may have some more tomorrow. I made a big dinner." The soup was followed by a crabmeat salad with mayonnaise Mexicaine garnished with avocado, a homemade raspberry sorbet, scalloped veal with asparagus and potatoes soufflé, Blue Stilton cheese with French bread and brandy Alexander pie. Jon had long since stopped saying anything of importance. He just let his senses take over and enjoyed a fine meal.

Finally, he could no longer resist. "When did you cook all of this?"

"I cooked this afternoon, of course. It's always difficult to make an interesting menu that allows me to be with my guests before the meal and not in the kitchen. Don't look so skeptical. I've entertained as many as twelve guests with dinners like this and done all of the cooking."

He grinned, and it occurred to him that he had been doing that almost constantly since he'd come for dinner. "I'm pretty damned sure that I'm a smart man. What other kind of man could find a woman who can run a big international institute, cook like this, dress a table like this, stage a scene like this, look like you look and kiss like you kiss? I'm clever as hell."

She gaped at him and then gave that full-throated, sultry laugh that he loved so much. If it made her happy, he'd do his best to keep her entertained with clever remarks. Suddenly, she sobered.

"Honey, what is it?" Like Dr. Jekyll and Mr. Hyde, she had undergone a complete personality transformation in less than a second. But as if determined not to backtrack, she took his hand.

"Let's move into the living room, have an espresso and some brandy, if you'd like some. Then we'll talk."

He didn't care much for that tone, but he couldn't let it dilute the joy that he felt. He walked into the living room, his heart racing, took a seat on the sofa and waited for her. She extinguished the candles and cleared the table. When she put the coffee and brandy on the coffee table and sat beside him, he sensed her tension and attempted to put her at ease.

"Sweetheart, you've made me feel something special tonight," he said softly.

She knew what he was trying to do. So she stroked his hand gently. There was no way to say it but to say it. "Do you remember when you called me from Oslo and I was in Washington visiting my mother?"

"Of course, I remember."

"Well, I was so miserable and so confused, mainly because of what was happening between us and because I hadn't heard from you that I unburdened my soul to my mother. She helped me to understand a problem that I've been groping with since I was twenty-one. I told you that there had been someone. I was no match for him. I was innocent and without experience, and I believed him when he said a thousand times that he loved me. I thought I loved him."

"You don't have to tell me this."

"But I do. I suffered a lot because of it. My mother told me that if I can't share this with you that you won't be able to repair the damage." She shoved back the threatening tears.

He pulled her into his arms, laid her head against his chest and rocked her gently. "She was right. Trust me, Haley, as you asked me to trust you. Tell me what you're feeling." When she couldn't continue, he made an easy guess and asked her softly, "How did he hurt you?"

She trembled from the memory of it. "He made love to me, or that is what he was supposed to have been doing. But I . . . it was my first time. He hurt me terribly, and when

I cried, he wouldn't stop. He . . . oh, Jon, it was awful."

"Did he prepare you for it?"

"What do you mean?" When he explained, she told him that nothing of the sort took place and that when she couldn't respond to Josh he'd abused her verbally. If she hadn't been so upset, she would have been shocked at the language with which Jon responded.

After a few minutes during which he stroked her back but didn't speak, he spoke with almost frightening calm. "Darling, the kind of man who would take what you gave him and treat it as that man did is not a man at all. He is sexually incompetent, and he hides it by blaming the woman who is honest enough to let him know that he didn't satisfy her. What he did was a crime. I want you to try and forget about it, because it had nothing to do with love."

"I know that now. In fact, the first time you kissed me, I knew that I had never been in love with anyone. Are you telling me that it doesn't have to be that way? I don't know, because there hasn't been anyone else."

"I'm telling you that it isn't that way, and it won't be that way with us."

She snuggled closer to him. How could she feel so at ease with this man? Until he'd

135

caressed her the night before leaving for Oslo, it had been seven years since she'd let any man touch her bare flesh. As usual, her mother was right, and she was glad that she told him. The music changed, and she searched his eyes to see if he remembered the song.

A smile lit his green eyes. Then they darkened to nearly black, and he swallowed with increasing difficulty as his breathing quickened. She knew he was in the grip of desire, and she did nothing to diffuse it.

CHAPTER 5

The music changed again and, still looking into his eyes, she sang along with Joe Cocker's recording of "When a Man Loves a Woman." As the song ended, he reached for another brandy to hide the quivering of his body. He ached from head to foot. The liquor would quiet the wild throbbing in his loins. At least, he hoped it would. But before he could down the drink she took the glass of brandy from his hand. He held his breath as she placed the glass on the table.

"Dance with me." She stood and held out her arms to him.

"Haley, be careful. This entire evening has set me back on my heels." In truth, it had been like a two-fisted blow to the gut. He took a deep breath, preparing for the battle that he had fought with himself for too long.

"I'm in love with you. I can't . . . Listen, if I don't leave here right now, you may never want to speak to me again."

"Why? You're not likely to say or do anything here tonight that will make me unhappy."

It wasn't in him to pretend either to himself or to her.

"I want you. I want to make love with you."

"I told you. You're not likely to say or do anything here tonight that will make me unhappy." He turned to stare at her. Then, seeing that her eyes were downcast, he stood and spoke softly, very softly.

"Baby, do you know what you just said to me?"

"I know, Jon. I . . . I know." Determined to show him that she merited his trust, she forced herself to give him a level look. "I want you to teach me what . . . whatever you think I need to know, and I'll try to be what you need."

He stared at her, speechless. She looked quickly away, and he knew that she was misinterpreting his silence. Yet he couldn't force a word out of his mouth. She stammered. "Well, I mean . . . You know . . . after what I told you just now, I thought we . . . I thought . . . I mean . . . you said you loved me . . . and . . . ."

He found his voice. "Honey, you can't know how moved I am. I've been under this shadow my whole life, and you've just told me that you want to bring sunshine into my life, that you want to make me whole. Do you wonder that I can't find words?"

"Maybe that's all it is, a wish. I don't have any experience. I just know that I want to be with you."

"Are you sure? This may not be easy for us."

"Yes. I'm sure. I know it won't be easy, but it will be wonderful," she told him. "I know that I haven't conquered all of my fears, but I know you'll help me, and I want to be with you. Show me how."

This was what he'd dreamed of with her. She'd softened since he'd left New York. Maybe it was that she loved him. She hadn't said so, but he felt it. He reached for her, no longer able to control his longing, his aching need to have her. But he had to go slowly. He couldn't risk getting out of control, and he had to remember that she was practically a virgin.

He took her face between his hands and looked into her soft doe eyes. What he saw in them humbled him. There was trust, an absolute certainty that what she felt and what she was about to do was right, was meant for her and for them. It warmed his heart, but it sobered him, too. Slowly, he lowered his head and his mouth found her parted lips. If he was hesitant and striving for control, she was not.

Haley opened her mouth the moment his heated lips touched hers and, as if driven by the winds that had cradled her ancestors, she moved into him with no thought for consequences. She thought only of loving him. His lips adored her, sweetly and tenderly, the kiss of a man deeply in love. But without knowing what drove her, she was impatient to feel the power of him, the force of his desire. She clasped her arms behind his neck, ran her fingers through his curly, golden hair. "Please, Jon, don't hold back on me. You know what I want."

"Tell me. Tell me what you want."

She ran her tongue around his full, sensuous bottom lip and sought entrance. She could feel the tremors that went through him, and for the first time in her life, she knew her power as a woman. Emboldened by the knowledge, she found his tongue and sucked it into her mouth, holding his head still while she took her pleasure.

He groaned, tightened his arms around her and, finally, she felt the full surge of his erection against her belly. She didn't try to suppress the shudders of desire that rocked her. His hands roamed over her body, caressing her everywhere. His lips adored the pulse of her neck, her eyes and her bare shoulder, and when she was nearly desperate for the feel of his mouth on hers, he ravaged her parted lips, his tongue setting her afire. His thumb had found its home on the nub of her nipple, caressing, rubbing and teasing. Weakened, she sagged against him. He broke the kiss.

"Haley, in my life, I've never wanted a woman as I want you right now. But I'll leave here this minute if you aren't sure that you want us to make love." When she raised her eyes to his, he saw that they were no longer that soft doe-like brown but obsidian pools of smoldering desire. She parted her lips and wordlessly beckoned him to her.

"I've been trying all evening to seduce you. I know I'm not experienced at this, so please don't make me beg. I intend for you to stay here with me tonight," she whispered.

"And will my accommodations be the same as last night?"

Clearly exasperated, she moved closer. With her left hand, she urged his head down until her lips found his mouth. Then she pressed her right hand firmly to his erect penis and stroked him, swallowing his groan until his body shook at the mercy of her loving hands.

Aggressively, she stroked him until he cried out. "Baby, what are you doing to me?" He knocked her hand away. Another second of that and he'd be out of control. He picked her up and carried her to the bedroom, his bedroom, the one in which he'd tossed and turned all of the previous night.

He set her on her feet and reached for the zipper of her dress. As the garment fell, he feasted his hungry eyes on the little mauve-pink silk things that served as underwear. She started to cover her nearly bare breasts with her hands, but he would not have it.

"Let me look at you. You're so lovely, so beautiful." He ran his palms over her full breasts and perfectly rounded hips, gazed at her olive skin against the lacy silk, and his mouth watered. He pulled her to him as gently as he could, but he kissed her ravenously, plunging his tongue into her mouth and simulating the age old dance of love. When she gasped for breath, he slowed down to see if he'd frightened her.

She showed her impatience by pulling at his tie and trying to unbutton his shirt. He pulled down her scant bra, spilled her generous breasts into his hand, opened his mouth and sucked the nipple of one. When

142

she cried out in passion, he sucked more greedily, his hand moving over her belly. After she managed to open his shirt, she kissed his chest, her hand playing in the golden curls that she found there. When she accidentally stroked his nipple and he gave an almost savage response, she leaned up, licked it and nibbled on it. She couldn't know that his reaction to it shocked him, that it was a new experience for him.

"Do that again. Yeah, like that. Yes, yes, just like that. Hell, woman." He had to stop her. He pulled back the covers, laid her on the bed and stripped her of her bra and bikini panties.

She lay there looking up at him, her breathing reduced to short pants, while he watched her intently as he slowly and deliberately undressed himself. Her gaze was glued to him, and he mesmerized her with his hypnotic movements as he peeled off his clothes. The sight of his fully erect penis amazed her, but she felt no disquiet. All she could think of was getting him inside of her.

"I never thought of men as being beautiful," she said, in barely audible tones.

He said nothing, leaned over her and, as if she were a lyre, began to play a tune on her body with his hands, fingers, lips and tongue.

Then, he lay beside her, painfully aware that their moment of truth had come. He teased one breast, then took it into his mouth and pulled on it in the way that he had learned was sure to tantalize her. Aware of her growing impatience, he caressed her inner thigh and, for the first time, claimed her — masterfully stroking her clitoris and massaging the lips of her vagina.

"Jon. Please! I'm going crazy. Why don't you get in me? Now!"

He rose above her and waited. In spite of his seeming reticence, she tried to capture him with her leg, but he resisted her. Then she realized that he was seeking permission to continue.

"Please, Jon, let me feel you inside of me."

"I want your word that if I hurt you even the slightest bit, you'll tell me immediately."

"You won't hurt me. Please, oh, Jon!" She stopped talking and leaned up to kiss him. When he didn't move, she took her hand and tried to force his entrance. She had the satisfaction of feeling his massive shudder.

"All right, love. I'll give you what you want, what we both want."

As they caressed each other with their eyes, he touched her warm, moist vulva with the crown of his penis. They both trembled from the shock of it. Seeing his hesitancy, she hugged him tighter. "I'm fine, honey. Don't worry. It will be all right," she whispered.

As he entered slowly, he watched her face, his heart nearly bursting with joy as a smile lit her face. But then she reacted as if in pain, and he attempted to pull away. She wouldn't permit it. Her willful, headstrong personality surfaced, and she brought her legs around his hips and held him prisoner in her embrace.

"But I hurt you. I saw it on your face, felt it in your movement."

"Please, Jon, give me a chance. Don't move away from me. I want you to make love with me so badly that I think I'll die if you don't. I like feeling you in me like this. Please give me more." He thrust slightly. "More, please, darling, give me more."

"Baby, I love you. You are the world to me. Please, don't be noble."

"I am not being noble. I know what I can take and what I want. Love me, please love me."

"I do. I do love you. But, baby, I've never been able to —"

She stopped him. "Don't tell me about you and any other women. I don't care who or what they were. They didn't want you as much as I do, and not one of them loved you like I love you. I want all of you, all of you, Jon Ecklund. I'm your woman, and I'm going to give you what you need, what you've missed all of your life." She raised her hips to him and placed her hands on his buttocks. He felt himself sinking into her. Frightened that he might hurt her, he tried to stop the movement, but he was so overcome with emotion at her words and at what was happening to him that his control was weak. He hugged her fiercely to him, loving her as he had loved no human being before.

"Haley, love, I don't know if you can take this. I know now that you want to, and it is enough."

Realizing how much of him she had accepted, he raised his head and looked at her. "Sweetheart, don't press any more. If I hurt you, I won't be able to live with myself." For the answer, she raised her hips, and catching him unaware, she grasped his buttocks in her hands and pressed him into her until he had no more to give. Then she wrapped both legs around his hips and began to move beneath him. He struggled for control. Unable to believe what he was experiencing, he stopped her and asked,

"Are you hurt? Are you all right? Tell me."

Her smile was the smile of love goddesses through the ages. "Darling, I'm in heaven." He kissed her tenderly and lovingly. But soon the love exploded into passion, and placing his hands beneath her hips, he began to thrust gently until in frustration she begged him for more.

"Please don't treat me like a doll. I'm a flesh and blood woman, and you can't hurt me. I want to feel your passion. I want to know your strength, your power. I want everything you have to give, everything."

It was his undoing. His control nearly shattered, he thrust into her as she had asked, giving what she was demanding, giving all of him. Then he heard her soft pleas, her soft cries.

"Darling, what's happening to me? I feel as if I want to burst. I'll die if I don't. Jon, Jon . . ." She was telling him something, and he got the message.

"Let go, love. Forget the past. It's you and me, baby. Trust yourself to me, and let yourself feel what I'm doing to you. Give in to me, and give up your fear of being exposed. Haley. Give yourself to me. Now, baby, now!"

And then as he felt her stiffen, her soft rhythmic pulsations began to grip him.

He encouraged her. "Yes. That's it. Relax and let it go. Yeah, that's it, love."

She flung her body up to him, and as he accelerated his movements, spasms exploded within her and rocked her from head to toe. Her thighs quivered and electric-like currents of sensation shot through her as he thrust into her. He had lighted a fire in her, and it threatened to consume her. She was sinking, dying.

"Honey, I'll die if this keeps up. I need to explode."

"And you will. Just let it go."

"Oh, my," she screamed, flung her arms wide and sank into the quicksand of his lovemaking.

The power of her response to him sent him out of control. "Haley. Haley, my love. My life." Giving her the essence of himself, he took her flying with him into sweet paradise.

As their passion slowly subsided and the sweet aftermath of love enveloped them, he held her to him. "If I could only tell you what you've given me. New life. New hope. If it never happens again, I've known complete fulfillment. Oh, Haley, I love you."

He didn't withdraw from her immediately but instead buried his face in the curve of her neck.

At that moment, they were one, and they both knew it. He raised himself upon his elbows and attempted to separate from her, but she held him tighter. "Stay. Please stay."

"But, honey, I'm too heavy for you."

"No, you're not. You're not too anything for me. You're perfect for me." He looked into her eyes and saw in their sated warmth that he had satisfied her completely and something else, too, but he was afraid to name it. He brushed her lips with his, trying to communicate the love that swelled within him.

"You can't know what has happened to me tonight. You can't imagine what I experienced with you, what you've given me. For the first time in my life, I've known the feel of a woman's breasts against my chest and felt her legs wrapped around me as I made love to her. For the first time in my life, a woman took all of me and I felt the convulsive tremors of her passion over the whole length of me. Haley, no woman has ever urged me to stay in as you did. Karen couldn't wait for me to leave her. Why? Tell me why. I've got to know." He kissed her gently, soft butterfly kisses, declarations of love, not of passion.

"I went with my instincts. I don't even remember what I did or what I said. I just knew that you needed me, and I wanted to be everything to you. I confess that it was difficult at first, but I made myself relax, and I could feel myself easing until after a while I wasn't a bit uncomfortable. Then, when you started to move, that powerful urge hit me. I hardly remember anything else.

"Let me tell you something, Jon. I'm jealous as hell of every woman you've ever touched, so please don't talk to me about any of them." She buried her face in his shoulder.

"My sweet, sweet Haley, you know that isn't necessary. But you haven't answered my question. Why? Tell me what you feel for me, I need to know."

"I love you. If I didn't, you wouldn't be here."

Jon thought his heart would burst.

He tired of resting on his elbows. "Would you mind if I move out now?"

"Why? You're right where you belong." Grinning, he nudged her nose with his.

"Yes, but if you've forgotten that you were practically a virgin, I haven't, and I don't want to make you sore."

"Do you mean that's all for now?" she asked, slowly closing her left eyelid.

"Are you saying you want more?" For an

answer, she wiggled suggestively under him. He held her still, knowing that he was already becoming aroused again.

"Sweetheart, I could love you all night and tomorrow, but it wouldn't be wise. Hold still while I move."

A grin surfaced around her lips. "Getting out ought to take you a while."

He noted that she said it with pure womanly pride. He separated them, moved over, lying on his back and tucked her to his side. She threw an arm across his chest, rested her head on his shoulder and was soon asleep.

But Jon lay awake, going over what had happened. For many years, he'd dreamed of, longed for and prayed for the experience that he had shared with Haley. If he couldn't have her for his own, he wasn't sure that he could make it. After what he had learned from DuPree earlier in the day, he wasn't optimistic about living in New York and running EIS from its North American regional bureau. Afraid that being a modern woman, she would sacrifice their relationship for her well-ordered life, he stared into the dark. Desperate.

Dawn found Jon wide awake after a sleepless night. He looked down at Haley's soft features, at the curtain of her silky black hair flowing over the pillow, over his arm and over his shoulder. Unable to resist, he bent to kiss her cheek, and his movement woke her. She snuggled closer to him, throwing her left leg across his hips. In response to her movement, he groaned, and she awakened.

"How long have you been like this?" she asked him, a full five minutes after having become aware of his aroused state.

"Good morning, love." It was a mild reprimand for not having greeted him as a lover should. She caressed his chest gently.

"You didn't answer my question. The truth, please."

"Well, if you insist on the truth, I'd have to say most of the night."

"Why didn't you wake me?" She moved away from him. "Why didn't you?"

"I wouldn't want to wear out my welcome," he said.

"You don't expect me to believe that, do you?" She moved farther away. "After last night, you'd have to be dense not to know that I want you, and you are not dense. We both know that the real reason you're suffering in silence is because you don't think it's worth going through all that again."

"Woman, what are you talking about?

Have you lost your mind? I lay here all night reliving the wonder of what I experienced with you. For the first time in my life, I feel like a whole man. And you pull out of my arms, turn your back to me and tell me that you didn't please me. Didn't I tell you how affected I am by what we shared? Haley, look at me. Look at me, and tell me you believe I'm lying here hard because you didn't please me. I thought I was being considerate. I thought you needed some time to recover from taking me the way you did. Baby, come here," he commanded, gruffly. "We're not enemies. We love each other."

She turned toward him, and he saw the single tear at the tip of her left eyelash stubbornly refusing to fall. "What is this?"

"I'm foolish. Oh, I don't even know how to tell you what I'm feeling. I'm not really sore. A little warm, maybe, so you needn't hold back on my account."

"That's impossible. You were as tight as a virgin. One of us has to be sensible. Come over here and let me hold you." She scooted into his arms and hugged him to her. But when her left hand wandered below his waist, he grabbed her wrist and held it.

"Do you know what time it is? It's six o'clock in the morning. Let's go to sleep."

His last thought before succumbing to sleep was that he wanted to get his hands on the man who had done such a hell of a job on her, completely undermining her self-confidence.

Haley sat on the edge of the bed that she shared with Jon the night before, holding a tray of coffee, toasted English muffins, brioche, fresh raspberries, sausages, butter and jam. She had barely touched the bed when he rolled over and looked at her. She smiled at his surprised expression. "The way to a man's heart is to give him coffee in bed." He laughed at her joke.

They spoke about inconsequential things as they ate the light breakfast. After a time, Jon looked at Haley, his face bearing a serious expression.

"We've talked about everything on earth but us. What about *us,* Haley?"

"What *about* us?"

"Are you serious? We love each other. We've spent the night in each other's arms, as close as two people can get, and you ask that question? If I never see another woman, I'm satisfied right now. You've given me more in one night than I have had in a lifetime. I'm a whole man. I love, and I am loved. I want a commitment."

He could see that she was stunned, and he felt a chill inside as terror gripped him.

"Why can't you answer me? I'm not interested in a one-night stand, Haley, and I hadn't thought that you were. You know how it is with me, how it has been with me. Did you think that you could give me the love and fulfillment that I have longed for all of my adult life, give me joy such as I had with you and just walk away? All I'm asking is that you and I agree to see if what we've found can be the basis for a life together. What about it?"

Haley opened her mouth, but the lips that could charm a miser out of his money would not utter a word. The sight of the pain etched on his face unsealed those lips.

"All right, but if I'm not free to see anyone else, neither are you." She nearly laughed at his look of surprise. "Well, that's right, and I'm serious, too."

"Yeah. I guess you are," he said with a half laugh. "I'll need a little time to get used to that sharp, bossy tone, but I'm sure that as time moves along, it will disappear."

She hugged him. "Not to worry. I'm as meek as a lamb."

Both of his eyebrows shot up. "Are we still talking about you? Look, baby, let's make the best of the morning. I'd like to get the eight o'clock SAS flight to Copenhagen to-night."

"I had hoped that you would stay longer. If you're leaving this evening, let's just fool around." She glanced at the bed. "No point in making that up. I mean —"

He rocked with laughter. "I think I've created a monster."

"Do you blame me if I want to make up for lost time? I'm almost twenty-nine. Look at the time I've lost."

He picked her up. Swung her around and hugged her. "You're precious. I'm beside myself with happiness."

"Me, too," she said.

"I'd better go first to my condo, get my things and close the place properly. I should be back here in an hour and a half. Okay?"

"Just don't make me wait too long," Haley said with a sassy grin.

An hour and a half alone gave her plenty of time to think. Was he planning to live in New York? And if he wasn't, what about her institute and the obligations she'd made to her financial backers? And would she marry a man who was for all practical purposes white, even though his mother was of African descent?

She decided to call a restaurant on Broadway, four blocks away, for their lunch, rather than use time cooking that would be better spent with Jon. He returned in a little less than an hour and a half, dressed for the flight.

"Until we picnicked in the park, I couldn't have imagined you in jeans," she said as they walked arm in arm to her living room.

"At home in Oslo, I wear them everywhere except to work." He sat down and lifted her into his lap. "You've had time to do some thinking. Any reservations about us?"

She stared at him. "Are you a mind reader? Well, I'm not sure that all my fears have receded, and I don't want to give up the institute."

"What are you afraid of? Certainly not me. Are you telling me that you can't trust me?" He ran his long, lean fingers nervously through his hair, and she could feel his tension.

"I know it's not rational, but it seems impossible that you could feel for me what you say you feel and that you won't tire of our, well, you know, of what we have."

He stared at her, unable to believe that she had actually said it. "I am not Josh or whatever his name is. You had me in your arms last night. Don't you know what went on between us? How can you let the words and callous act of a self-centered, incompetent man interfere with our relationship? And what was that about your career?"

"Nothing, I guess, since you'll be coming back here in a few months. If I have children, I still intend to work."

"Of course I don't expect a woman with your education and competence to give up working. The question is what and where. I learned yesterday that my father wants to retire altogether. I'll know for certain when I speak to him, but there's little chance that Jason DuPree would misinform me. My guess is that I'll have to take over as CEO, and that means working out of the home office. And while I'm at it, I may as well tell you the rest. Dad wasn't able to put out the fire completely in the Southeast Asia office, because there's something shady going on there. I'll be headed back out to Bangkok at the end of next week."

She bristled. "You're telling me this as if you're putting me on notice that I have to make adjustments to your moves. I said I love you, but I didn't say that I was your hired servant."

Jon looked at her, silently and for a long time; his eyes flashed a warning if she'd bothered to see it. But she didn't.

"If you want us to be together, we're both

going to have to make some compromises." Evidently, realizing that anger was serving as a protective cover for her, Jon opted for self-control.

"Haley, I'd best tell you a few things about my business affairs. EIS is only one division of a conglomerate owned by my family and managed by my father and me. Svend, my brother, is a dentist. His only concern with the business is the medical instruments manufacturing company that we own. He manages the technical, but Dad takes care of the business end of it. We have a few oil wells, some woolen mills and we make blank CDs and DVDs. EIS is the only division of the company, Ecklund, Ltd., that requires daily hands-on management in the Oslo office by my father or me."

He got up and began pacing the floor. "If we'd had more time together, maybe our decisions would be easier. God knows I want you with me. You alone can decide what to do. Don't give me an answer now. Take some quiet time and consider the possibilities, your options and mine. I can't give you up, Haley. I've waited too long for you." He stopped in front of her, reached out and caressed her hair. "You're my life, woman, and don't forget it."

Her options! She gave him a list of reasons

why she couldn't leave IISP and follow him to Norway. He stopped in front of her, leaned over, grasped her by the shoulders, pulled her up to her full five feet ten inches and towered over her. "I told you that I'm not giving you up and I mean it."

"Then do something!"

"Oh yes, I'll do something, all right." He clasped her head firmly but gently, held her and then crushed her lips with his, putting all of his frustration into the kiss. He opened his mouth and ran his tongue around her lips. She opened to him like a flower to the sun, and he plunged his tongue into her mouth, and with its movement, he told her what he wanted to do.

All she could think of was the power of his lovemaking, the way he'd moved inside her and the thrill of bursting wide open in his arms. She wanted it again. She wanted him. She slid her arms up to his shoulders, sank her fingers into his thick blond hair and took some for herself. When she heard him groan, she had a moment of uncertainty and tried to pull in the reins. She didn't want to be at the mercy of his passion. She wanted some control. But he clasped her buttocks tightly to him, letting her feel the fullness of his powerful arousal, and she was lost. Moaning and sucking on his tongue, she moved against him, undulating her body, telling him what she wanted. He picked her up and carried her to her bedroom.

"You're the only woman in my life, and I intend for you to remain the only one so long as I live." As he said it, he unzipped her dress, unhooked her pink lace bra and let her full breasts spill into his hands, a perfect fit. Then he kissed her, first gently, softly, tantalizingly sweetly, but when he felt her impatience, he sucked a nipple into his mouth, gripped her to him and let her feel all of his hurt, frustration and fear of losing her. His kiss held all the desperation, uneasiness, longing and conflict that he felt.

She braced her hands against his chest, wanting to look at him, but he held her too closely for her to read his expression.

"You're squeezing me."

"I'm sorry, love." He relaxed his grip, surprised that he'd been holding her so tightly. "I'd sooner hurt myself than you. Haley, don't you know how much I need you?"

"Just . . . it's just that . . ." she whispered.

"Shh, love. This is our time, and I want to make the most of it . . . for both of us. There's no telling when we can be together again." He pulled off her strip of a panty,

161

kissed her belly, hip bone and every spot of flesh as he slowly peeled it down. When he reached her black silk triangle, she shivered. Slowly and deliberately he stripped the tiny garment from her ankles and threw it onto a chair. Then he draped her left leg over his shoulder and pleasured her with his tongue until she moaned.

"Jon, don't. I mean, oh —"

"Baby, let me love you the way I want to. Let me have you." He sucked and kissed until she began to undulate wildly. Then he let her feel the pressure of his tongue thrusting in and out. As he caressed her, he felt the tension building in her and felt his own passion escalating. Knowing that he couldn't tolerate waiting much longer, he moved away from her abruptly. She cried out in frustration, but he soothed her.

"Be patient, sweetheart. I finish what I start. You can depend on that!" He undressed slowly, his eyes never leaving hers. And finish it he did.

CHAPTER 6

"Will the time come when I don't have to be cautious?" Haley asked Jon.

"Maybe, but until that happens, I'm always going to make certain that we both remember." He kissed her beloved face, her eyes and the pulse at her throat. When he felt her begin to stir, his kisses became bolder, feeding his passion until he sensed she was ready.

"Get in me. Now. I want you in me." Staring into his passion-filled eyes, she took him in, glorying in her ability to fulfill him.

"Are you all right? Are you having any pain?"

"Stop worrying. I feel incredible. Just let me have you. Oh yes, yes." She wrapped her arms and legs around him, accepted him completely and closed her eyes.

"Look at me, Haley. Open your eyes and look at me." She forced herself to look at him, and what he saw made him gasp. "You are mine, do you hear me? *Mine.* You are my woman. Do you understand that? Answer me, Haley." He wasn't moving, just holding her and gazing with fierce intent into her eyes.

"Yes. And you are mine, Jon Ecklund."

He kissed her, letting her feel his love, his need and his fear for their future. She rocked beneath him, wild and frantic.

"Stop pampering me. I need to feel your strength and power," she pleaded.

And then, she got what she wanted. It began as a flush beneath her feet and moved up her body to become a quivering volcano at her core. And then she felt the powerful pulsation of her inner muscles around him and a sea of passion engulfed her.

"Help me," she screamed. "I'm dying."

He followed her shattering release. "Haley. My love. My life," he moaned and then gave her the essence of him. Spent, he collapsed in her arms.

She held him until he had to leave her in order to catch his flight. "No, sweetheart. I don't want you to go with me. You'd have to come back from Newark alone. Just be here for me when I get back."

After their long and, for her, painful good-bye, she fell across the bed and went to sleep. Dawn found her tangled in the bedding.

Days later, Haley looked over the text that she had drafted and, satisfied, told Amy to prepare it in final form. Her trip to the reservation should take her mind off Jon and her dilemma about their future.

The drive from the airport to the reservation was long and hot. Haley was tired and hungry by the time she arrived there. But as Gale cautioned her, she went directly to the old chief to pay her respects and to ask his blessings and guidance. He seemed disappointed that she didn't speak her tribal language, but he treated her graciously.

"Welcome, my daughter. I am pleased to see that you care for your people, even as it distresses me that you have lost your heritage."

"No, sir. I know where I come from," she retorted, bristling. "I know who I am, and I am proud of my heritage. My parents made certain of it. I understand the language of our Comanche people, even if I do not speak it."

"The Comanche are fortunate. *Our* educated young people do not often find their way back to us and, when they do, our circumstances make it difficult for them to help us. But this is a time for rejoicing, not sorrow. I am glad that you have come to us. We must educate our children here, where their roots are. We want our children to learn to use computers, to know world history, science and languages, but we also want them to know and appreciate their own culture, their heritage, the ways of their people," he said.

She told him of her plans for the children. "Will you recommend a good children's storyteller? One hour each day will be devoted to stories of the old ways and to tribal history." The idea clearly pleased the tribal elder.

"Yes, my daughter, I have just the person. Her name is Birdsong."

With the help of the old man and Birdsong, Haley found two other excellent teachers. They located a suitable classroom, furnished it and began to change the life prospects of twenty-seven eager little girls and boys.

As she boarded the plane for New York, she should have been buoyed by her success, but what she felt was discontent.

"Dammit," she said to herself. "I can get along without him just as I've been doing for almost twenty-nine years. No, I can't. I love him, but I don't want to change my life, and it looks like he can't change his."

"Why are you so somber?" The voice of the woman sitting next to her broke into her thoughts.

"I didn't know I was," Haley said.

"Would you like to read this?" the woman asked, handing Haley a paperback novel. "A good whodunit ought to take your mind off whatever's bothering you."

"Thanks. A distraction might be just what I need right now."

The woman put down the magazine she'd been reading and turned to Haley. "If you don't make up your mind, he will certainly make it up for you."

"He? Did you say *he?*"

"I sure did, and I am absolutely right." She put the paperback in Haley's lap. "When you've had as many lovers as I've had, you can spot a woman with man trouble a mile away."

Haley turned to get a good look at the woman. She was good looking and obviously wealthy. "Are you married?"

The woman shook her head. "No. After the second try, I realized that I was the problem. I like to have my way, and I hate compromising. Now if something doesn't suit me I pack up and leave. I keep it simple." She ordered a scotch and soda from a passing stewardess. "Don't worry, for the rest of the flight I plan to mind my own business and read this magazine. Have a nice flight," she said and smiled. Then, with drink in hand, the older woman turned her attention to the magazine in her lap.

Haley couldn't help smiling as she mulled over the woman's advice. A little while later, she closed her eyes and slept.

The taxi moved away as Jon fitted his key into the front door lock of his parents' home. It was his home, too, for now. He'd keep the condominium in New York City and the house in upstate New York, but if he stayed in Norway — and it appeared that he might — he'd get a place of his own. Walking up the stairs to his room, he wondered why he continued to postpone putting some order into his personal affairs. It wasn't like him to tolerate so many loose ends. He dropped his bags by the door. The house was empty. His parents were in Spain and wouldn't be home for another week.

He changed into a pair of old jeans and his favorite red-and-black shirt and went down to the kitchen to see what he needed from the store.

He decided that he would not let his mind dwell on Haley while he was here. She was his whole world, but she had issues and was having a problem seeing past them. He made a list, got on his ten-speed bike and peddled along the rolling hills peppered with the last yellow and golden hues of his beloved autumn. If only Haley could see it with him. If only she could experience the beauty of his ever-changing lakes and hills as he saw them. He sped up and was soon at the supermarket.

As he walked the aisles searching for oatmeal, his favorite breakfast, he recalled that Haley brought him breakfast in bed. Only his mother had done that and even then only when he was sick. Haley seemed to enjoy making him happy.

"Oh, hell!" Why couldn't he stop thinking about her? What if she decided that her institute was more important to her than he was? What if she wasn't in love with him after all? What if he was the real problem?

Look at the mess he'd made of his own life, he thought. First, Karen, who was completely self-centered and selfish and now, Haley, the woman God had made for him, but who seemed scared to death to give up control and take a chance with him.

He'd peddled the eleven miles home without realizing it. After putting his groceries on the kitchen table, he polished a red apple and walked out onto the back porch, eating as he went. He stood there, looking at the forest beauty and the words of a song that he didn't even know that he knew floated through his mind. "All alone. Just me. Me and my memories." Suddenly, he wished that he had a dog. What a strange thought, he mused. He'd never wanted pets. It occurred to him that what he needed right then was a commitment from Haley. He didn't dare ask her yet to marry him for fear she'd say no. But did he need a dog?

Instead of rushing to the nearest pet store, Jon went into the library and dialed his brother, who lived in the heart of Oslo. They spoke amiably for a few minutes and agreed to meet for lunch the next day.

Haley's staff broke into heavy applause following her report on Reservation Project #2, which she'd just begun. But as she trudged to her office, she experienced not a heady feeling of pride but feelings of resentment. Resentment of what? Of whom? She refused to run home to her mother every time she encountered an emotional roadblock. She was a grown woman, a prominent executive with consequential and far-reaching responsibilities. But, she needed a friend. She needed Jon.

"Yes, Amy."

"Nels Andersen is on the line."

"I'll take it. Hello, Nels. It's good to hear from you. What's up?"

"How about lunch? No, it's too late for lunch. I didn't realize the time. Are you free for dinner?"

For a moment, she didn't respond.

"Haley, are you there? If you're busy, we could make it another time."

"Sorry, Nels. I'm not busy this evening, but I doubt I'll be good company."

"You and Jon have a spat?"

"I wish it were so simple. We haven't had a spat, but we may be headed that way. Okay. What time?"

"I'll pick you up at seven sharp. Put on something red. I've got a hunch you're in the dumps."

"Seven it is. See you then." She hung up. Dumps? She was in a deep hole, and she saw no way out of it. She was not going to quit the institute and live in Norway, and there was no other way for her and Jon to be together.

Nels greeted her with a kiss on the cheek. "You didn't wear red, but you're still gorgeous."

"Good Lord, Nels, you're exactly what I

needed right now."

The maître d' greeted Nels warmly and seated them. The waiter arrived and asked their preferences for predinner drinks. Nels wanted an iced vodka and dubonnet blonde cocktail, and Haley requested her usual cotton picker.

"One perestroika and one cotton picker coming up," the waiter said.

Nels raised one eyebrow. "What on earth is a cotton picker?"

She laughed. "Southern Comfort over snowballed branch water."

"Damn!" They both laughed heartily.

She loved Nels's company. He was so natural and unaffected. Not a few times she had wondered why he was still unmarried. He was a kind man, warm, unpretentious and capable of genuine friendship. If she had a sister, she thought, she'd match her with Nels.

"Wool gathering, love?"

"Sorry. Why are you single, Nels?" She could have bitten her tongue. "Oh, Nels, forgive me. That is none of my business."

He forced a weak smile. "I want to get married, but just *once,* Haley. She'll be a woman who wants what I want and need — a home in the country, five or six kids, dogs, cats, maybe some chickens. I just don't want

172

glamour."

He'd stunned her, and she showed it. He went on. "Jon and I have a lot in common in that respect. We're both pretty deep," Nels said. "What's going on between you two?"

"We love each other, Nels, but I don't see how we can make it."

"You're kidding. That man is deeply in love with you. I've never known him to be as happy as he was the day that he was go- ing to have dinner with you at your home. What's holding you back?"

"Too many hurdles. Unsolvable prob- lems."

"Such as?"

"He's moving to Norway, and I'm staying here. I can't give up the institute, because its survival depends on me, and Ecklund, Ltd., depends on him. His father is retir- ing."

"Well, I'll be damned. But you do love him?"

"All the way to my soul!"

He digested that for a bit. "Is that all that's wrong? Your careers?"

"Isn't that enough?"

"Frankly, hell no. You think about it. I know both of you. You were born for each other, and you're going to spend the rest of your lives looking for clones. What a bloody mess! Honey, look for a compromise. There is always an acceptable one somewhere."

"That's what he says, but I don't see it. And, Nels, if we don't stop talking about him, I'm going to be too miserable to eat."

Jon met his brother for lunch as planned at an elegant old inn just above the city. Its simple beauty was enhanced by its idyllic site on the side of a mountain amidst centuries' old spruce and elm trees. "Are you really going to move back home, Jon? I never would have thought it possible."

"Unless you want to run Ecklund, Ltd., I don't have a choice. Dad has retired, and you damned well know it."

"I'm sorry, old man. I can hardly sustain an interest in the technical side of Norse Medical Instruments. You know that periodontics is the only thing that gives me an A-1 high."

"I know how it is with you. I didn't mean to get testy, but this comes at an awful time for me. I've got a girl in New York, and she can't leave there."

"What are you telling me?"

"For the first time in my life, I've got a woman who completes me, makes me a whole man, who complements me in every

174

way. And I have to give her up."

"Are you saying what I think you're saying?"

"Depends on what you're thinking. It's something personal that I've never discussed with you."

"Look, man, I'm not stupid. I know more than you think I do. In the eleven months that you and Karen lived at home with us, my room was next to yours. Are you saying that this woman in New York is . . . well, what you need?"

Stunned, Jon simply stared at his younger brother for several moments.

"I think she was made just for me," Jon said at last.

Svend had worried about his older brother ever since he'd guessed the root of the problem between Jon and Karen, his former sister-in-law. And he was overjoyed that Jon had finally found his mate. It sickened him that Jon might lose her as soon as he had found her. "If I were in your place, brother, Ecklund, Ltd., could go straight to hell. What's her name?"

"Haley Feldon."

"Sounds familiar, very familiar." He thought for a moment. "Is she some sort of expert on East Africa?"

"Not particularly, but you might have seen

an interview she did in Nairobi on women's health, broadcast on EIS a few months ago?"

"Yeah. That's it. A tall woman with eyes like a fawn and jet black hair? She's one hell of a beautiful woman. And smart, too. *That's your girl?*"

"She was for a brief while."

Svend released a sharp whistle, something not expected in the city's most elegant restaurant. Heads turned.

"Get to work on it, man. She's worth it. She appeared to be rather swarthy. Is she Spanish or what?"

"Her father was African American, and her mother is Native American. She is beautiful, but that's not why I love her. It's her sweetness and patience, her tenderness and loving acceptance of me." His voice took on added huskiness. "I . . . I really love her, Svend."

"I know you do, and you've just told me that she loves you."

"Yes, but . . . but so what? I can't ask her to give up something so dear to her. I don't dare." He looked away.

Svend dropped some bills on the table and rose quickly.

"Come on, let's go," Svend said as he dropped some money on the table and stood. He draped his arm around his older brother's shoulder, assuming the posture that Jon invariably took with him, and steered the way to the side exit.

"I was thinking that, since you're here you could give me a course in the management of the company. I could schedule my office appointments for mornings only or for three days a week and spend the rest of the time with you, learning the business. Hell, the only thing I know about wool is that it comes from sheep and about crude oil is that it's greasy. I haven't treated you fairly, Jon, letting you assume the entire burden of the family business. You could work in New York, and when I get into trouble here, I could call you or send you an email. I like being a dentist, but hell, I don't *have* to be one."

Jon turned to look at his younger brother. "I can't accept such an offer, Svend, but I'll always remember that you made it in good faith, and I know what it cost you." He poked Svend playfully in the shoulder. "Thanks, but, no thanks. I don't resent my responsibilities, Svend. I resent losing my woman, and if I stay here, I will. I can think of solutions to our situation, solutions that would take a little from each of us and that would make us both richer. But when we

last discussed this, she can't think of any —
not one. Until she can envisage even a small
compromise, I can't see a future for us."

"I'm sorry."

"So am I, Svend. So am I."

Jon loped down the stairs the next morning
to the smell of coffee. At the foot of the
stairs, he saw luggage with the airline tags
still on them and quickened his steps to the
kitchen where he knew he'd find his parents.

He greeted them in Norwegian. "Did you
get here last night or this morning?"

"Last night," his mother said, examining
him closely. They told him about their vacation, his father's retirement and their decision to take a lengthier vacation in the
spring.

"It's good having you here, Jon," Erik said.
"I'd better unpack."

"You're not happy," Inger said the minute
Erik left the kitchen. "Didn't she respond
to you?"

"Oh, yes. I told her everything, and she
didn't bat an eyelash. She gave me heaven
on earth, everything I could want. She is
perfect for me."

"But what? Is she married?"

"Good grief, no, but her work is there,
and mine is here. I can't ask her to leave

what she's worked so hard to accomplish."

"But there must be an acceptable compromise."

"I don't have much hope that we'll find one."

"Tell me about her." He told her about the woman he loved, unaware that his face glowed as he spoke of her.

"She sounds wonderful. I want to meet her."

After her talk with Jon, his mother went to her room and quietly telephoned Svend. "Your father and I are going to give Jon a big party for his thirty-fifth birthday, and I want to invite his girlfriend in New York. Please get the address for me, but don't tell Jon why you want it."

"All right, Mom, but do you think that's a good idea?"

"Trust me. It's a perfect idea."

Haley lifted the receiver. "Sky! How are things?"

"Things are great. Looks like you're catching up with me. That job you did on TV last night will get your institute some powerful backers. Congrats!"

"Coming from my big-shot journalist brother, that's a super compliment. Thanks."

"I'd have thought you'd be jubilant after that level of success. Uh-oh. You're not mooning over this guy Mama mentioned, are you?"

"I'm not mooning over Jon. We've got issues, and I can't figure out how to . . . he wants me to compromise, and I can't."

"Stubborn as ever, I see. Jon who?"

"Jon Ecklund. He's in Europe, and I —"

"You're not talking about *the* Jon Ecklund, the CEO of EIS, are you?"

"One and the same. I love him, but I can't give up all I've worked for and freeze my butt off in Oslo for the rest of my life."

"I hope I'm not hearing straight. There usually has to be some compromise in a relationship. Get your act together, Haley. He's worth the effort. See you." He hung up.

She didn't let Sky's mild reprimand bother her. A man would see things a man's way. She fished through the morning mail and blinked several times when she saw the name Inger Ecklund on the return address of a letter. With trembling fingers, she tore it open, praying that it didn't contain bad news about Jon. She read it.

Dear Haley,
Jon's father and I are giving him a party

to celebrate his thirty-fifth birthday. In his father's family, it is a tradition to celebrate the thirty-fifth as the midway point between birth and old age. You've given Jon so much happiness that I know he won't enjoy this momentous occasion unless you are with him. Please say you'll come and spend a few days with us. We want so much to meet you. Please let me know as soon as possible. My phone number and email address are below. Looking forward to meeting you. Warmly, Inger Ecklund.

Haley's lower lip dropped. She leaned back in her desk chair, speechless — but only for a minute. She opened her computer and sent Jon's mother an email.

Dear Mrs. Ecklund,

Thank you for inviting me to Jon's birthday party. I'll be happy to share it with him and his family. I'm looking forward to meeting you and Jon's father. Please let me know the particulars. Warm regards, Haley

She telephoned her mother. "Jon's parents are giving him a birthday party, and I'm invited. It occurred to me that when I'm

181

ready to leave Oslo, you and I could meet and tour Scandinavia together. You always wanted to go to Finland, and this would be a good opportunity."

"At least you're accepting the invitation. I'd love to tour the region with you, but this is a lot to digest, Hessy. Let me know the dates, and I'll see if it works."

Half an hour later, Haley received an email from Inger Ecklund giving her the dates and telling her that Jason DuPree would be in touch with her to arrange her transportation. Should she go there without knowing Jon's thoughts about her visit? She emailed him saying, among other things, that she hoped he'd come to New York soon.

"I've been trying to manage that, sweetheart," she read in his answer, "but I've been overwhelmed. I can't wait until I see you again. I love you, Jon."

It disappointed Haley not to see Jon waiting for her when she reached the baggage area at Gardermoen Airport, even though she knew he was unaware of her visit. Then to her surprise, she saw Jon walking toward her. When the man got closer, however, she realized that he was too old to be Jon or his brother and had to be their father.

"Welcome, Haley. I would have recognized

you anywhere. Jon has given us a flawless description of you. We've been looking forward to meeting you." She smiled and extended her hand to him, but he ignored it and hugged her. Feeling the genuine warmth of the embrace, she returned his embrace wholeheartedly.

"I'm glad to meet you, too, Mr. Ecklund. Jon didn't tell me that he is the very image of you. I've never seen such a likeness in my life. When you were still some distance away, I thought that you were he."

Erik Ecklund's smile suggested a treasured memory. "Wait until you see Svend and my wife together. That's a shocker, too."

As he gathered her bags and they left the airport, Haley wondered how Jon would act when he discovered her surprise visit. She also felt uncomfortable about staying with Jon and his parents for a week when her relationship with Jon was so poorly defined. Besides, she didn't think it would be in good taste to go to bed with him in his parents' house.

Noticing her apparent unease, Jon's father took her hand gently in his. "You belong with us, my dear."

What would it be like to awaken in the same house with Jon, eat breakfast with him, maybe even dinner for the next week and not know the joy of his arms or the sweet ecstasy of holding him within the heat of her body? If she hadn't been envisaging impending torture, she might have laughed aloud.

Haley hadn't pictured Jon's mother in her mind's eye, perhaps because he'd said little about her, other than that she was African American. He hadn't said anything about his family home. When the limousine arrived at the Ecklund home, a large two-story, white stucco building with red shutters set well back from the road in a thicket of spruce and elm trees, she was both surprised and pleased. Looking at it, one didn't think of wealth but of family and warmth. A large red chimney adjoined either side of the house, and curtains, drapes and old-fashioned shades could be seen at the windows. The grounds were beautifully landscaped, and lovely evergreen shrubs surrounded the house.

Inger Ecklund opened the front door and walked gracefully down the steps to the driveway. She looked past her husband as he alighted from the car, eager to see the woman who had illumined the life of her firstborn. The two women smiled simultaneously, and Haley walked into the arms of the woman who had given life to the man

184

she loved. After they embraced, they stood back to look at each other, and it shocked Haley to see tears in Inger Ecklund's eyes.

Then the woman smiled again. "Welcome to our home, Haley. I'm hoping that you and I will be able to make the most of this short visit and get to know each other. We are very informal, and we don't dress for dinner except on very special occasions. I'll show you to your room." As they walked up the wide stairs, they spoke amiably and without strain.

As tall as Haley, Inger Ecklund's rich-brown flawless skin, dark sparkling eyes, fashionably cut short black hair and svelte figure would be the envy of any fifty-six-year-old woman.

From the window of her room, Haley gazed at the beautiful trees and the river beyond them and thought that Jon could never live in a city like New York. There wasn't enough peace and quiet. Anyone raised in that environment needed tranquility. There was much about Jon that she didn't know and much that she might never know.

"Well, what do you think?" Erik Ecklund had draped his arm around his wife's shoulder.

185

"I'm not sure. She's very warm, and she loves him."

"How do you know?"

"I could tell by the way she greeted me. It was almost as if she were hugging Jon. She greeted me with love, Erik. Maybe they'll find a way. They have to. He's out of his mind with the fear of losing her."

"Do I detect a reservation?" Erik asked.

"About her? No. I'm just praying they're not foolish enough to lose each other."

"Well, we'll just have to wait and see. Are you going to like her?"

"I already like her," Inger said. "I couldn't dislike her if I worked at it. What time is Jon coming home?"

"He and Svend should be home in about half an hour," Erik said and laughed.

"What mischief have you been up to?"

"Mischief? Me? Woman, surely you jest. I just can't wait to see my self-possessed elder son's face when he finds Haley here. Also, I can't wait to see him cope with sleeping with only a wall between him and the love of his life." He grinned wickedly. "She seemed a bit uneasy about something, and I suspect she knows that if she's around him all the time, she'll be putty in his hands."

"Shame on you!"

Suddenly Erik sobered. "Fun aside, I want

my son to have that woman. I like everything about her and, believe me, love, I am not above a little meddling."

Jon walked into the house ahead of Svend and walked into the den where he expected to see his parents. After a little small talk about his trip, Inger asked Jon to get something out of the guest room for her.

Impatient with his mother's request, he took the stairs two at a time. He was surprised to find the door to the room closed. He opened the door and stood speechless in the doorway.

Through the slightly cracked door, he saw Haley lying on the bed asleep. His breath shortened. Then he felt a tightening in his groin, and in spite of his willpower, he couldn't stop what he knew was coming — a full erection and a blinding, all-consuming desire for her right then, right there.

How could this be? he wondered. After spending about ten minutes in his room, he took a few deep breaths, went back and knocked on her door.

"Yes?"

"May I come? I want to look at you, to know that you're really here."

She rolled off the bed, rubbed her eyes with the back of her right hand, kicked a shoe out of the way and padded to the door. "Hi, honey. Your folks wanted to surprise you," she said. "So far my visit has been wonderful. But I have missed one thing. I haven't been kissed in ages."

Her bold invitation was all the encouragement he needed, and he pulled her to him and parted his lips above hers. She broke the kiss quickly. "Do you think this is a good idea here in your parents' home?"

He thought for a minute. "It'll be very cool toward evening. Put on something warm and comfortable, and let's go for a walk. I'll put a thermos of coffee and a couple of sandwiches in my backpack, and we can have a snack somewhere along the riverbank. I'll meet you downstairs in ten minutes." He gave her one more quick kiss. "I can't believe you're actually here."

As they stepped out of the back door, he called to his father, who was collecting walnuts from beneath a tree. "We're going for a walk, but we'll be back before dark."

"It's a wonderful evening for a walk there, but don't forget that the bears fish along the river."

"Trust me, I won't."

Haley hadn't experienced an encounter with a wild animal, but with her hand tucked in

Jon's the prospect didn't bother her. "Do you ever fish here?" she asked him. "It may sound trite, but I want to know everything about you."

"Svend and I have spent many hours on these banks with strings and bacon, and we caught plenty of fish." The wind picked up, and when she bunched her shoulders, he took off his woolen scarf, wrapped it around her neck and zipped her jacket up to her chin.

"Let's sit here where we can see the fjord in the distance."

He poured a container of coffee and handed it to her along with a salami sandwich. "How long can you stay? I know you're here until my birthday the day after tomorrow, but after that, what?"

"My mother is going to join me Friday, and we're going to tour Scandinavia. She's always wanted to see Finland, so I suggested we go there together."

He put the thermos on the ground and stared at her. "Would you let your mother come here and not give my family and me the opportunity to be gracious to her? I want to meet her. Why can't she come to my birthday party? What's her telephone number?"

"But —"

189

"But nothing. What would she think of me? If things go my way, she'll be my mother-in-law. What's her name?"

Haley stared at Jon, her mouth a gaping hole. "Gale, Gale Feldon," she said.

"Don't look so shocked, Haley. We love each other. You're my whole life, and you must know it. Don't you expect us to get married?"

"Uh . . . a woman can't take that for granted. I mean —"

Jon knelt on the ground before her and took her hands in his. "I love you, Haley, and I will until I stop breathing. I'll be faithful to you and take good care of you and our children. Will you be my wife?"

"I . . . uh . . . I love you, too, but, Jon, there are so many things to iron out. I mean, you have to be here, and I don't see how I can leave the institute. My backers and my staff are depending on me."

"You're prepared to give up all that we've found, and —"

Her temper surfaced, and she fought to control it. "So it's up to me. I have to make the compromises and the adjustments. I've studied and worked hard, sacrificed to create the institute. What are you suggesting — that I just walk away from it?"

He looked at her for a long while, stood

190

and then put the thermos in his backpack.

"Let's go." He didn't reach for her hand to help her to her feet, nor did he touch her as they walked back to his house. "See you at dinner," he said once they were inside.

After a nap, Haley awakened to find the afternoon sun filtering through the beige curtains of her room. She stretched luxuriously. Music. Which one of them played a harmonica? she wondered. She didn't wonder long, however, as the lilting bars of "If I Loved You" floated to her through the open window. Jon! She rushed to the window, not bothering to don a robe. Just as she opened the curtains, the song came to an end, and he looked up, as if sensing her presence.

They stared hungrily at each other, not moving, not speaking. She forgot her state of undress, and he was powerless to hide the flagrant evidence of his arousal. They remained in that near catatonic state until a shift of the wind sent a cold gust of air through Haley's window, making her conscious of her near nudity. She turned quickly away.

He swore savagely. She hadn't been wearing a thing but those two scraps of pink that she called bra and panties. Suppose somebody else had been out there. He didn't want any other man looking at her body. He didn't want other men looking at her period. He frowned. What the hell was he to do? She hadn't given him the right to be possessive. The hell she hadn't! In a venomous mood, he stormed into the house, almost knocking his mother off her feet.

" 'Scuse me," he offered, without stopping to learn what damage he might have done. She only glanced at him, as if acknowledging that it was only the beginning. He met Haley on the stairs and stopped. Thankfully, she had dressed.

"I didn't know that you play the harmonica. And so well, too."

"Yes, I play the harmonica. Please excuse me." He walked around her and continued up the stairs.

CHAPTER 7

Responding to the pain in the region of her heart, Haley leaned against the dining room table for support. Seeing and feeling the barrier he had erected, she hurt. She wanted suddenly to touch him, to have him touch her. She wanted him to hold her, to need her. She wanted his hands and his mouth all over her. She wanted him to love her. And as she envisioned him in her arms loving her, the heat spiraled through her body and settled in her loins. So intense was the experience that she caught her breath and closed her eyes.

He was looking right at her, right into her large doe-like eyes, heard her gasp and knew what she was unable to hide. All he had to do was pick her up and carry her to her room and he could be inside of her in minutes. Yeah, he could have her, but for how long. He wasn't into self-torture. She wasn't his and didn't want to be except, he thought bitterly, when her libido tricked her. The hell with it.

He stepped around her. "Excuse me, Haley." He could almost feel the shock travel through her, but he didn't look back. At dinner that evening, they managed the necessary smiles and to treat each other civilly, but they both knew they hadn't fooled Jon's parents and Svend.

Walking by the river the next morning just after sunrise, Haley thought back to her meeting with Svend. In appearance, the two brothers had only height and physique in common. Whereas Jon was fair with green eyes, Svend had the dark hair and startling grayish-brown eyes of his mother. Svend's personality was enigmatic. One thing was certain: Svend was fiercely protective of his older brother, at least where she was concerned. She knew that Jon's parents liked and accepted her, but in Svend, she sensed a near-surface current of hostility. Like a genteel adversary, he'd greeted her with interest and not a little curiosity, but he didn't accept her and hadn't bothered to hide it. What had Jon told him? Everything, or nearly everything, she decided, for Svend had disliked her before he ever saw her.

After some consideration, she concluded that she didn't know how to handle Svend's attitude toward her or even if she should try.

The next morning, she picked up a sturdy, dry branch and used it for a walking cane as she trudged up a path. She was so deep in thoughts that she hadn't heard anyone approach.

"So you've found the wisdom tree, have you?" She looked up to find Svend standing two feet away.

"The wisdom tree?"

"Yeah. Jon spent half of his youth sitting under this tree thinking. If you're looking for answers, they're not under this tree. And if you're half the woman he says you are, you'll find your answers in your heart."

"What entitles you to rudeness? Since you obviously dislike me, keep your views to yourself." She stood to leave.

"I don't dislike you. I simply have a low tolerance for women who toy with men."

"How dare . . ." But she was speaking to the air. He had turned and left. "Damn," she muttered and headed slowly back to the house, her thoughts in disarray.

"Oh, no." She said to herself when she saw Inger climbing a slight hill and coming in her direction. She didn't want the company of any human being other than Jon.

"Isn't it a beautiful morning?" Inger asked. "I'm so glad we're meeting here. I wanted to take you sightseeing, but I don't want to interfere in Jon's plans. Have you been over to the river?" She took Haley's hand. "Let's sit over there. I love to hear the water rushing by."

They sat on a wooden bench that didn't have a back, and Haley was aware that Inger had not released her hand. "Do you ever miss home?" she asked Inger.

Inger turned to face her. "Didn't Jon tell you? I'm a Norwegian citizen, so I *am* home. Erik married me two days after we graduated from the University of Pennsylvania and brought me home to meet his parents. That was more than thirty years ago. Erik and our sons envelop me in so much love that I don't miss my relatives in the States. My parents are gone, and I never had any siblings. Mother and Dad used to visit once a year, and I went to the States once a year, but after they passed, I had no interest in going so regularly.

"I'm happy here, Haley, because the man I love is here. When I became a citizen, I changed my name from Inez to Inger, and that was more than a symbolic gesture. I fully intended to enjoy my Norwegian citizenship. Of course, I am still a United States citizen, and I will never give that up. Does this question bother you about your relationship with Jon?"

Haley blew out a long, tired breath. "It's more than that. You hadn't begun your career, but I'm deep into mine." Feeling the weight of the problem, she shook her head from right to left. "He's such a wonderful man."

Inger eased her arm around Haley's shoulder. "That's why you will find a way." They walked back to the house, discovering that they had in common a strong love of nature.

Although she had Inger's support and compassion, the gap between her and Jon seemed to grow wider by the hour. For the remainder of the day, every time she caught him looking at her, he looked away. If she entered a room and he was there alone, he left as soon as possible. He greeted her civilly, as he would any very casual acquaintance. She tossed in bed that night until the top sheet was wrapped around her. She hated the bed. She hated the night. The night, those awful hours when she needed him most, when he slept a wall away. When she could hear him walk, hear him run the shower, hear him get into bed. She wanted to scream.

In desperation, she crawled out of bed, pulled on a pair of jeans, a T-shirt and sneakers without socks and started toward the door of her room. She glanced at her travel clock — one o'clock in the morning. Five long, dreadful hours before daylight. Walking quietly down the stairs, groping in the dark, she stumbled at the bottom step when she was suddenly blinded by a light. "Are you all right, Haley?" She glanced up to see Jon's father.

"Yes, I'm fine. I didn't think anyone else would be up at this time in the morning," she said.

"Why *are* you up?"

"I couldn't sleep."

"Yes. And from the looks of you, this isn't the first night, either. This is a big house, Haley. But it isn't so big that you and Jon can't find each other. Go back upstairs and figure out whether what's keeping you apart is more important than being together. Believe me. You don't have to be Einstein to master that equation. Look into your heart and accept what you find there. Good night, my dear."

She stood staring at his back as he walked up the wide staircase, looking for all the world like Jon. At the top, he stopped and looked down at her. "A woman doesn't have to be smart to get a man who is in love with her. She only has to love him. I mean really love him. Sleep well."

She flicked off the light, and with tears blinding her, she walked slowly up the stairs. *Good advice, but how do you show a man you love him, if he won't even look at you?*

Alone in the den the next morning, Jon leaned back in his father's desk chair and stared at the ceiling. *Why, God, did you give her to me and then dangle her in front of me like this?* He rested his head in his hand. He needed some fresh air. Suddenly, it occurred to him that, unless she'd gone shopping, he was certain to run into her. "Damn," he muttered as he opened the door and almost knocked her down in his rush to get to his room, change clothes and head for solitude on his bike.

"Hi, where are you going in such a hurry? I thought you were spending the day at the office."

"Did you, now? I'm going for a ride on my bike." He started walking around her and headed for the stairs.

"In that case, I'll have the house all to myself. Your parents have gone to a party at the Hansens over in Drammen and won't be back until late."

He stumbled momentarily as he climbed the stairs, started on up again and then stopped.

"Why didn't you go with them?"

Haley didn't miss the carefully controlled irritation in his voice, nor the fact that he didn't look her in the eye.

"I wasn't invited."

"Where do you think you're going?"

"To my room to get a bubble bath and a nap. Any objections?"

Damn her! He didn't want to know what kind of bath she was getting. He didn't want to think about her lying there in that pink tub covered with nothing but scented bubbles. He turned sharply up the stairs and toward his room, walked in and closed the door somewhat more loudly than he'd planned. Feeling the tightness in his groin, he headed for the bathroom and another of the countless number of cold showers he'd taken since she'd been sleeping in the room adjoining his, because he'd been able to hear every move she made, damned near every sigh she uttered. It had to end. He couldn't tolerate it.

He stepped out of the shower, rapidly dried off and not bothering to wrap a towel around his waist, stepped into his bedroom and stopped still. She stood before him wrapped in a shimmering red silk kimono, the jet black silk of her hair flowing nearly to her waist. She didn't look like a self-confident siren, either. She looked like a vulnerable, frightened woman, but he ignored that.

He was a player with the advantage, coming in for the kill. It wasn't fair to her, and he knew it. But the agonizing ache that he felt from head to foot wouldn't allow him fairness.

"What are you doing in here?"

Apparently jolted both by his nakedness and his total disregard for it, she was momentarily speechless.

"Isn't it obvious, Jon?" Nervously, she rubbed her flattened palms up and down her silk-clad hips. He tensed, every muscle on sharp alert, feeling as if his very life was on the line. Look at her, he thought, a tidbit that any healthy male would give his eye-teeth to nourish himself on. For a second, he wanted to throttle her — standing there knowing what she looked like and knowing how she affected him. And oh, so soft, so . . .

Haley saw him struggling for control and knew that, with his genius for mastering himself, he might turn her down. And she didn't know how she would bear the humiliation. All she'd thought about when she made up her mind to go to him was that she loved him and needed him, that she wanted to show him love and tenderness. She couldn't turn and run now. Too much was at stake, and she might not get the courage again. Something had flashed momentarily in those green eyes — hatred, desperation, she didn't know which.

He took a step forward. "Nothing is obvious with you, Haley. You're a living, walking riddle, a bloody enigma."

"Jon, we've meant too much to each other to have it come to this." Dammit, she wouldn't let him see how she was hurting. She wouldn't let him know that he might as well drain the blood from her veins as reject her summarily without an iota of tenderness or even the semblance of warmth and caring.

"Come to what?" He raised an eyebrow, daring her to accuse him of anything. He wanted to see her squirm.

"Come to what?" he repeated.

"To name calling and abuse."

"You think you can bat your big eyes and I'll fall at your feet? Snap your fingers and I'll come running? Turn it on when you want it and turn it off after I satisfy you?"

he ground out brutally. "That's what you think? Well, dammit, I've got news for you, woman. I am not a slave to my sexual needs or to you. I was celibate by choice for five years, and I could have gone another ten."

"All that self-control you're talking about took place before you were ever inside of me. You're mine now, Jon Ecklund, just as I'm yours. *And I want what's mine!*"

The truth obviously stung. He moved toward her, thunderously mad. She stood her ground. She was going to have him, the consequences be damned. She should be scared, she thought, but she wasn't.

"So you want what's yours, do you? You want me in your bed, so long as I tiptoe out of there before anybody in this house gets the notion that Dr. Feldon made love with me, right? And you'll play it cool tomorrow and the next day, gracious and ladylike, making plans for your precious IISP — that is, until your libido acts up again. No thanks," he snarled, scornfully and, forgetting that he was in his own room, he started for the door. But she got there first.

"May I please pass, Dr. Feldon?" She didn't move or speak. Less than half a foot separated them. They looked at each other. So close. She wanted to touch him, to sift her fingers through the hair that covered his chest and tapered to a vee just above his proud manhood. She wanted her hands on him. And she knew him and every vulnerable spot on his body. If she could just get her mouth on his nipples, he'd be hers. Involuntarily, her hand went to her left breast, as if to sooth the ache there. She swallowed with difficulty, and her tongue slowly rimmed her top lip as desire gripped her.

"Haley, don't do this," he warned her.

The caution was just soft enough to give her courage. She didn't heed him. She lifted her left hand to caress his beloved face, her eyes mirroring her love for him. Shaking, he grabbed her wrist, but whatever he'd intended was lost. The feel of her skin after so many weeks of remembering what it was like, the scent of her hair, of her woman's body lowered his resistance. Weakening, he turned her hand and kissed its palm. She groaned aloud and reached for him. But he was immediately on guard, his anger resurfacing, and he attempted to back away from her. But she caressed his penis with her right hand and squeezed the aroused length of him. He groaned aloud and took her roughly to him in a powerful surge of anger and with the churning need of a starving man looking at food well out of his reach.

He ground his mouth against hers in a brutal, punishing kiss, but she was gentle and pliant, giving sweetness for ire, softness for his harshness.

She knew that he was angry, that he was being too rough, that he was showing neither tenderness nor mercy, but she didn't care. She knew that no matter how angry he was, when she finally got him inside of her, she'd make him forget about it.

She caressed his naked shoulders and back, stroked his bare arms, knowing that he needed her gentleness. He broke the kiss and looked at her, aiming to shatter her with angry words. But she ran the tips of her fingers over his face, soothing his scowl. She kissed his neck, his shoulder and finally, she nuzzled his nipple. His groan could be heard almost throughout the massive house. She held him tightly, fearing that he might break away from her. Instead, his hold on her tightened. Warily, she glanced up at him, fearful that she was losing him. He stared blankly at her, revealing nothing of what he was feeling, yet pinning her tightly against his aroused flesh. When her lips parted involuntarily in want of his, he uttered a curse, picked her up and dumped her on his bed. He stood naked over her for what seemed to her like hours, and then he slowly unloosed the sash of her kimono, exposing the ripe beauty of her nude body.

She hadn't known what to expect, but as he leaned over her, she saw the tumult raging within him. And then she saw that as his eyes slowly swept over her, his anger and internal conflict were conquered by his love for her, the evidence of which leaped into his eyes. She opened her arms, reaching out to him on a level that only lovers understand. She moved over to make a place for him and clasped him to her. She held him, stroked him, kissing his neck, his shoulder, his chin. He didn't close his eyes, wouldn't give in to the avalanche of passion that she was creating within him. But she had him where she wanted him, and they both knew that she could not lose.

Haley knew that the ball was in her court, and she didn't hesitate. He lay beside her on his side, his right hand draped over his head. She sat up and very gently pushed him onto his back. She sighed in relief, knowing that she had gotten him into the supine position only because he had decided to cooperate with her. She leaned over him, looking into his eyes, those normally serene but now turbulent eyes that always shook her composure. He didn't smile, didn't move, didn't encourage her.

She stroked his face gently, hiding nothing of her feelings. Her insecurity, anxiety, vulnerability and fear were there for him to see, as was her love for him. He was deeply moved, seeing for the first time the depth of her feelings for him and about him. She laid her head on his broad chest and felt him tremble. Encouraged, she moved her face slightly and let her lips brush his nipple and was rewarded with his involuntary jerk. When she sucked it into her mouth, he groaned as if in agony. Having had no experience in the purely physical seduction of a man, she didn't plan her moves, merely followed her instincts and his reactions. She climbed on top of him, pinning his arms to the bed as she did so. She knew that he wasn't her prisoner and that he was letting her have her way with him. She started slowly down his long, big body, kissing and stroking her way.

She felt his trembling and knew that she was getting to him. She squeezed and stroked him, rubbed her face over his iron-tough belly, and then ran her tongue around his navel. He began to move in ways that suggested he was struggling to remain still. She laid her face upon the soft yellow hair at the apex of his thighs, while she stroked first his hips and then his belly again. Running her hands up the insides of his thighs, she reached her goal and cupped him possessively. That made him groan.

Now, he wasn't still, and he still wasn't resisting her. He grabbed her shoulders and tried to pull her up, but her lips went to the crown of his penis and her tongue slid down its massive length. "Haley, stop teasing me. Take me, for God's sake, *take me!*" She parted her lips and sucked him into her mouth. Then she loved him and as much of him as she could manage. He writhed beneath her, moaning in sweet agony. Suddenly, he jerked beneath her, startling her. But it was enough to shake her hold on him. She was rapidly bringing him to the pinnacle, and he wasn't going to permit her to do it, especially since he well knew that she didn't know what the consequences would be.

He pulled her up to him, wrapped her in his arms and nuzzled her ear, while he fought to dampen the fires she had lit within him. He'd been totally at her mercy, almost helpless under the awesome onslaught of her inexperienced explorations. The way she'd squeezed and stroked him . . . and her mouth, her lips and tongue.

When he began the gentle stroking of her breast, she moved away just enough to see his face. Amazed by the love that she saw reflected in her beloved's eyes, she brought her arms to his shoulders, love and desire fighting for dominance within her emotions.

"Love me however you need to."

Deeply moved, he didn't speak but cradled her head in his hands and found her lips with his own. But the sweetness of the kiss quickly erupted into steamy passion, and he buried his face in the valley between her breasts, stroking her, kindling her rapidly escalating hunger.

He fully intended to make her want him as much as he wanted her. As he continued to caress and stroke her breast, he hoped that she would soon become impatient and start asking for what she needed. And at last she did.

"Jon! Jon . . . ooooh . . ."

"What do you want, baby? Tell me what you want." She began to twist and to writhe. "Tell me what you want."

Too shy to say the words, she looped her hand behind his head and brought her nipple to his lips, but he didn't accommodate her.

"Tell me. I want you to be able to tell me what you want me to do to you."

"I want you to take my breast into your mouth."

"And do what?"

"Oh, please. S-suck my nipple."

He suckled first one and then the other breast. Then as she was moving out of control, he brought his hand to the folds of her vagina and dipped his long fingers into her slick heat. He saw that she was ready for him, and his chest expanded with pure male pride.

"Please, darling, now. I need you," she moaned. Still he stroked her. "Jon, please."

He moved over her, parting her thighs with his knee. "Listen, baby, you will have to obey me. I don't have any protection for you, so when I move out, don't stop me. Do you understand?"

"Yes, yes, I understand. Now, please."

With control made possible by love alone, he eased gently and slowly into the warmth of her, shattering the remnants of her reserve as she bucked beneath him. "Easy, love, don't rush to it. It will find us." He began a gentle thrusting, but she would not have it and begged him to give her his power, the strength of his manhood. When she wrapped her long legs around his hips, ran her hand between them and found his nipple, she had him. And he gave her what she wanted and what he needed. He had nourished her passion before, had seen her lose herself in him, but he was totally unprepared for her response to the powerful, yet tender thrust with which he loved her. Staring into her face, he watched her soft doelike eyes darken from brown to black. And as the pulsing and squeezing of the sweet passage that sheathed him escalated into violent clutching, he saw her spin out of control.

"Jon, oh, Jon, love me. *Love me!* Oh, Lord, hold me, Yesssss . . . !"

He saw her beautiful face contort and felt the jerking motions of her body as she literally came apart.

It was too much. He didn't want it to end, didn't want a return to cool reality. But when her rhythmic pulsing began again, he felt his own approaching ecstasy. "Haley, baby, release me. I can't hold out any longer. *Let me go, baby!*" Instead, she crossed her ankles above his buttocks and tightened her arms about his shoulders. "I can't. Not yet, not now. Please, please . . ." With all of his remaining strength, he pulled away from her and collapsed on top of her, unable to protect her from the impact of his weight. For a few minutes, he knew total peace and contentment. Had any other man ever found such bliss, such sublime ecstasy in his woman's arms?

Slowly, his breathing steadied and he was able to lever himself up on his elbows. What had they solved? Nothing. He gazed into her eyes. She had him besotted, all right. But he wasn't hypnotized, and he would damn well keep his own counsel and put on the brakes.

"Do you realize that you could have gotten pregnant? I did my best, but I could have missed, you know. You promised to cooperate, but you didn't. Why?"

She brought a hand up to his face and gently caressed his cheek,

"How could I? With you, just now, I felt as if I eclipsed the sun. For as long as I live, I will know that, at least once in my life, I transcended time and space. My mother once told me that if I trusted you and let you, you would take me to heaven with you. She was right. And no one, not even you, can take it away from me."

"You didn't answer my question. I think I moved in time, but you could be pregnant, you know." The glowing smile that lighted her face shocked him. She pulled him to her and hugged him fiercely.

"Does that mean that you're willing to marry me, make a home with me, share my life and raise my son with me?" It was almost imperceptible, but he felt her sudden stiffness, her certain withdrawal. "Damn you!"

His bare feet hit the floor. He headed for the shower.

"Jon, please . . ."

"If the answer isn't yes, you've nothing to say to me. How do you think you have the right to use me for your stud?"

He turned and walked back to the bed. She'd pulled the sheet tightly around her shoulders.

"You're a great lay, sweetheart, but you're not Krazy Glue. I can and will walk away from you. And don't bother to gloat over that little stunt you pulled, either. Any woman with hands can get a man to want sex, if only temporarily. And you do know what to do with your hands, baby."

"Jon, please, you couldn't mean that," she said softly.

"Like hell I don't! I told you that I wouldn't let you use me. You've got some gall playing with me this way. What kind of a woman are you? You want my body until you're satisfied. Seems like you'd even like to bear my son. But you don't want me," he snarled. "Find another fool." He strode back toward the bathroom. "And please be gone when I get back in here," he threw over his shoulder.

■ ■ ■ ■

As she crawled out of Jon's bed, she heard
the bathroom door slam behind him and
then the shattering of glass and knew that
he had sent his fist through the bathroom
mirror. Should she offer assistance? He
could be cut and bleeding. But she didn't
have the right to touch him, so she quietly
closed the door and went to her room.
There, she fell across the bed wanting to
cry, but the tears would not come. Half an
hour later, she heard him leave. He'd passed
right by her open door as if she no longer
existed.

It wasn't over. It couldn't be. He was
everything to her, and she wouldn't give
him up. "Please, Great Spirit," she prayed,
reverting to her roots, "make him forgive
me. Make him see that I love him."

She replayed the afternoon's events in her
mind time and again, forcing herself to view
her own behavior with merciless honesty.
Gradually, she accepted his verdict that she
had indeed used him, that she had taken
advantage of her knowledge of him and his
needs, that she had been selfish and self-
centered. Finally, exhausted, she slept lying
across the bed in her silken kimono. And

there she stayed until Inger Ecklund walked softly through her open door well after midnight to turn off the light.

Awakening from a restless sleep, Haley knew at once that the gentle hand upon her shoulder did not belong to Jon. Turning so that she lay partially on her back, she looked up into the compassionate eyes of the woman who had given life to the man that she loved. She was beyond embarrassment.

Inger Ecklund sat beside Haley and, after judging her mood, she folded the grieving young woman in her arms.

"When did you last eat?"

"I don't want food, Mrs. Ecklund."

"Please call me Inger. Neither you nor Jon ate dinner. I know what I left in the kitchen. Put on something warm, and come with me."

"Thank you, but I can't call you by your first name. You're Jon's mother, and that seems disrespectful. Maybe I'll go down and get some tea."

"I'll go with you." Haley put on a woolen robe, and together, they went to the big family kitchen. But once there, she couldn't swallow the tea.

"I know you don't want to talk about it. And I know that whatever happened was serious. But I also know that my son has never loved any woman as he loves you. So whatever the problem, you can make it right."

"No. He's finished with me. I tried to show him how much I wanted him, but he feels that I took advantage of him, and he was right. I had no right to seduce him. It gave him hope, led him to expect a compromise, but I had none to offer."

"But you love him. I know it."

Haley didn't hesitate to confirm it. "Oh, yes. And I'll love him as long as I breathe."

"I'm as certain as I am of my name that the two of you are right for each other. When you both hurt badly enough, when the pain and the loneliness become harsh enough and unbearable enough, you'll find a way."

Hadn't Amy said those identical words? "Perhaps we'll both gain some perspective after I've gone back to New York. I can't bear to face him."

"Haley, use your considerable intelligence. He will feel your presence just as much as you'll be aware of him. And as for seducing him, well, that's been permissible to women since Eve. Next time you do it, though, try to be a bit more artful."

She looked at Jon's mother and absorbed the warmth coming from her. "You know, I think I could learn to love you, really love you." Together, they climbed the stairs as Inger draped her arm around the woman that she hoped would bear her first grandchild.

On that Monday morning, Jon sat in his office thinking back to Saturday afternoon and Haley. He'd left her and ridden hell for leather up and down the rolling hills on his bicycle, trying not to feel, not to think as a growing sense of desperation crowded in on him. Why couldn't she see and accept that they belonged together. He had punished that bike until darkness overtook him. Then he'd shoved his bike into the garage, gotten into his car and gone into Oslo to see Svend. Perhaps it was fortuitous that Svend was out, because he had been forced to go back to his parents' home and to greet Haley at breakfast the next morning.

She had smiled as if they were in perfect sync, showing no remorse, no apprehension, wariness or unhappiness. Yet, he was certain that she had been crying aloud when he'd left the house on Saturday. He still had a lot to learn about women — especially that woman.

A few hours later, he leaned lightly against the marble column near the baggage carousel in Gardermoen Airport. Haley had said that her mother would be easy to spot, because the two of them looked very much alike. Somehow, he doubted that. Haley was unique. He spotted a woman who had to be Gale Feldon, and she was looking directly at him. He'd figured she'd be good looking, but he wasn't prepared for her stunning presence. As he approached her, he saw the smile spreading across her face. She extended both her hands to him. Holding her hands, he stood there looking at her and knew that he was going to like her tremendously. She spoke first.

"Jon, I'm so happy to meet you at last. And thank you for coming to get me."

"Welcome to Oslo, Dr. Feldon. I've been eager to meet you," Jon said with a smile.

"How is Haley, or perhaps I should ask, how are you and Haley?"

"Fine," he answered, coolly. "She's working hard at raising the status of IISP."

"Humph. And what about the two of you?" They hadn't moved.

"She's got that on hold or maybe canceled. I'm not entirely sure which. Come on. Let's get your bags." But she remained there, not moving and still holding both his hands.

"Do you love her?" She searched his eyes

and he didn't doubt that she saw the truth there, even before he answered.

"Yes, I love her. I can't even describe what I feel for her. She's given me more than I thought I would ever have."

"Good heavens! You've given her as much as she's given you — more, for all I know."

Jon didn't hide the fact that she'd stunned him.

"From everything my daughter has told me about you, you're a fine man, a gentleman, and I've been familiar with your work as a journalist for years. But, my dear, haven't you learned that when it comes to her personal life that Haley never moves until she's pushed out of her comfort zone? You give her too much space. Stop being so considerate. There are times when a man can be too much of a gentleman, and this may be one of them."

Jon gaped at her.

"Is she pregnant?"

"Good grief, no," he sputtered, "or at least, not that I know of."

"Why not?" She was grinning, conspiratorially. "There's more than one way to slice bacon, you know."

He stared at her for a long minute. Then he released her hands, threw his head back and gave a loud laugh. He lifted her up and swung her around. Then he set her on her feet, hugged her gently and kissed her on the cheek. Surprised at his uncharacteristic display of emotion with someone he didn't know, he stepped back, took her hand and led her to the baggage carousel, overjoyed at her insight and wickedness and her cheerful acceptance of him.

"Jon, Haley was a wounded bird until you healed her. I don't want to see her erect that protective shell around herself again. I know what it is to find heaven on earth with a man. I found it with Jack Feldon, and I want it for my daughter. She's stubborn and tends to load the world on to her shoulders, as she's doing with IISP, but as I once told her, I'll place my wager with you any day."

Jon considered himself fortunate to have had Gale Feldon to himself at their first meeting; she made him feel good. He'd bet his share of Ecklund, Ltd., that she wouldn't spend thirty minutes away from her man unless it was forced on her. Why couldn't Haley be like her? He eased his father's silver Mercedes to a halt in front of his parents' home and walked around to open the door for Gale. As she stepped out of the car, he couldn't resist hugging her. As he did so, he looked over her shoulder to see

Haley and his parents observing them from the doorway.

When his mother walked onto the lawn to greet Gale, he smiled at her. "Mom, I think I've brought you a sister. Gale Feldon, this is my mother, Inger Ecklund."

The two women embraced as if each knew that they would be friends. Gale looked from Jon to his father and tried unsuccessfully to control a grin. "Are there any more twins in the family?" she quipped.

"You may decide that for yourself when you see Svend and my wife together," Erik said, extending his hand to Gale.

Haley couldn't understand why the scene surrounding her mother's arrival had saddened her so much. She sat quietly throughout dinner and the lively conversation that followed. The family clearly loved Gale. And this charismatic, entertaining and totally engaging Svend was totally new to her. He had always treated her with cool detachment. Jon appeared oblivious to her, but his father had watched her carefully all evening and was clearly looking for an opportunity to draw her out.

Erik went to the piano. "Got your harmonica on you, Jon?" he asked. When Jon nodded, he began to play and sing a folk song. Jon joined him.

"Gale, do you sing? You, Haley?" Erik wanted to know.

Gale's hands went up, palms out. "I only sing for my enemies. Haley is the only one in our family who has a voice."

Jon looked at Haley as if he knew she'd back out of it. And she did try several excuses, but Erik would not accept them. "Come over here and sing with me," he ordered in a gentle voice. He played some Beatles ballads and Haley sang along, but when Jon began to play "If I Loved You" on his harmonica, she bolted for the stairs and went to her room.

"Come in," she said, thinking that it was her mother, and she stared, openmouthed, when Erik Ecklund walked into her room. "Haley, my dear, I'm sorry if my thoughtlessness caused you distress. I had observed that you were somewhat melancholy, and I only wanted to cheer you up."

She managed a weak smile. "Have a seat," she said, pointing to the chaise longue.

"May I spend a moment with you?" he asked her.

"Of course. I always enjoy your company."

"Yes. But just now, you would prefer to be alone. I know that you are distressed because our families seem to blend so beautifully and you cannot take the step that would make it official and lasting."

She sucked in her breath, horrified at his ability to read her feelings. But before she could answer, he continued speaking.

"I know. No one wants to be transparent. And you aren't. But I've lived a long time, and I understand human nature. Every woman would want her in-laws to love her and her family. There is love abundant for you here, but you cannot fully embrace it. My dear, most people never know the love, the mutual chemistry and the passion that exists between you and Jon that should unite you forever. If the two of you waste it, you are throwing God's precious gift right back at him. Rest well, but I hope you'll think about what I've said."

Haley was still sitting on the side of her bed when her mother entered the room. "I'm not going to say a word about tonight, Hessy. But now that I've met Jon, I'm almost sorry that your father and I ever sent you to school. Stupidity would have been ample excuse for you. The two of you are crazy about each other and going steadily insane because of it. If he were mine, I'd be with him if I had to swim the Norwegian fjords. Get some sleep. And get rid of your adolescent dreams of marrying a man like your father. Jack Feldon was my man. Jon

Ecklund is yours. He isn't black, has yellow hair and doesn't sing tenor. But by damn, he's yours."

"I don't think about that anymore, Mama."

"Thank the Lord. Good night." She closed the door and went to her room.

Jon knew an old tradition in his father's family was the celebration of a family member's thirty-fifth birth, and for his parents' sake, he pretended to look forward to the occasion, though not without some remorse. After his party the next day, Haley and Gale would leave, and although he had avoided Haley ever since she'd seduced him in his room, he'd nevertheless gained some comfort from her nearness, from seeing her every day, knowing where she was and that she was all right. He didn't want to think about the lonely days to come.

If he didn't escort her to the party, he would be rude and she would be mortified. If he did, he'd have to touch her, smell her, look at her . . . and he'd want her. So what, he thought, was there a waking minute when he didn't want her, didn't need her? He used his cell phone and called Svend.

"Dr. Ecklund here."

"Ecklund *here,*" he playfully corrected

Svend. "Got a minute?"

"For you, anytime, big brother. What can I do for you?"

"May I count on you to escort Gale to the reception, or are you planning to bring someone?"

"Yes to number one and no to number two. Although, I had thought that you would prefer to bring both of those beauties yourself. You *are* planning to escort Haley, aren't you?"

"I don't have much choice." It was out before he knew that he was going to say it. He remembered, almost regrettably, that in a moment of despair he'd told Svend something of his Saturday afternoon encounter with Haley.

"Jon, you know my feelings on the matter of you and Haley. But no matter what you say or why she did it, you sure as hell enjoyed having her take you. Don't be so self-righteous, man. She'll do it again, if she has any brain. And you will enjoy it again. I'll tell you for the last time, go after that woman with everything you've got. She's worth it."

"That's strong talk from the man who treats her as if she's a deadly virus. Why is that, Svend?"

"Oh, I like her, but I believe she should

fish or cut bait. I let her know it, and I don't intend to let her forget it. If she thinks that I dislike her, it's fine with me," he said.

"I've always known you had my back, but if I haven't said it recently, thanks, little brother," Jon said and hung up.

Jon and Svend sat in their parents' living room sipping brandy and awaiting their dates. They were both dressed in black tuxedos. Hearing the approach of women's shoe heels, they both stood.

Gale preceded Haley into the room, a vision in a strapless gown of yellow sequins, her black hair in a fashionable French twist. Jon could hardly wait to see Haley. When she did appear, immediately behind her mother, he groaned audibly. She wore a fiery red twin to her mother's dress, a strapless, sequined, hip-hugging sheath slit to mid-thigh. Her jet-black hair billowed softly around her shoulders. When she walked into the room, her glance found him and rested on him and him alone, unwavering, caressing him and telling him that she had eyes only for him.

She stared up at him as if hypnotized, and when she moistened her lips, he felt as if he was about to become unraveled. He couldn't take his gaze from her and was unaware that he was slowly moving closer to her. She knocked the wind out of him, and he could feel the ache starting to grip his loins.

He took a deep breath and managed to recover his wits.

"Ladies, you both look beautiful tonight," he said to the women. Taking each of them by the arm, he walked to the sofa.

Svend feigned offense. "Hold it, buddy. You're over in my territory." He took Gale by the arm and walked with her over to the ceiling-high window, where a full moon now lighted the sleeping gardens. "If you weren't going to be grandmother of my nieces and nephews," he proclaimed loudly, "I'd try to make some time with you. You are all that a man wants in a woman and some to spare," Svend said as he winked at Gale.

Laughter spilled from Gale's throat at his daring prediction and outrageous flirtation.

"Ah, Svend, you're a darling, a scoundrel and a wonderful man, and you've probably just sent those two into a coma." Then she added, "You look awfully good, too. In fact, I dare say that Haley and I will be the envy of every woman at the party."

Had she looked at Haley and Jon, she would have seen her daughter's furious blush and Jon's stricken look of desperation. Just then, Inger and Erik entered the living room, interrupting their chatter. Jon looked around him, wishing for all his worth that this could be truly his family along with the children that Haley would give him.

At the first dance, Jon appeared at Haley's side.

"Dance with me."

Though she was surprised at his action, she didn't hesitate. She went into his arms, moving her body close to his. She looked into his eyes and saw his want and his need, and she knew he felt the shudder that went through her. What was she going to do? She had to get out of there, away from him. She started to move away, but he held her.

"You owe me at least this one dance," he ordered harshly.

She continued to dance with him in silence, and after a few steps she moved closer to him once again and laid her cheek upon his shoulder.

He glided them toward the gold anteroom, where he moved away from her and walked over to the window, facing it. He turned to look at her, and the expression of sadness that he saw on her face melted his heart.

Rather than strangling her as he'd wanted to do back there in the ballroom, he wanted to hold her, to comfort and protect her. Protect her from what? With that ammunition she carried around, somebody had better protect *him*. The thought cheered him. He walked over and draped his arm loosely around her shoulder.

"We're a pair, aren't we?" He'd said it sadly and so softly that she was unsure whether he expected a response. She longed for him to hold her, to love her. Too miserable for caution, she leaned against his shoulder. He hugged her gently and then put space between them as quickly as he could. "We're killing each other, Haley."

"Yes, I know. Is love always like this? Sometimes I wish I had stayed ignorant of what it's like to care so deeply."

"I agree," he said out loud. But now was definitely not the moment for any confessions, true or otherwise, he thought to himself. "Listen, Haley, are you hungry? Let's go find something to eat."

She looked up at him, seemingly bewildered by his change in mood.

"Oh, and Haley . . ."

Her expression indicated that she anticipated the worse.

"Let's keep some space between us."

"That ought to be easy," she said. "I'm flying to New York Monday morning."

"You and Gale aren't going to Denmark, Sweden and Finland?"

"I talked her out of it. I want to go home."

CHAPTER 8

Svend and Gale watched them as they walked back into the ballroom.

"One thing is certain — they weren't kissing out there," Svend muttered, needlessly. That was already obvious to Gale as well as to Jon's parents. And the seemingly immovable barrier between the two lovers cast a pall over the group as they seated themselves at the head dinner table.

After a sumptuous meal, which none of them was able to enjoy, they drove home in silence. In the car, Erik Ecklund patted his elder son on the shoulder. "Happy birthday, son. You're a fine man."

His father's compliment pleased him, but it didn't ease his pain. As they entered the foyer of his parents' house, he pulled Svend aside. "Can you see them to the airport?"

Svend raised one dark eyebrow and leaned against the pale green marble mantel. "Yeah. I'll do it, but how will it look if you don't go?"

"I'm beyond caring how anything looks. I'm only sorry that my actions might offend Gale."

"Yeah. Well, just let me know what time they're leaving. See you tomorrow." After a long, hard look at his brother, Svend bade them all good-night and headed for the city.

Almost as soon as Haley entered her room and began to remove the shimmering red gown, Inger Ecklund knocked on the door. "There's a call for you and Gale. Push the button marked three."

She thanked Inger and paused, wondering who would call them at midnight.

"Hello," she said, unaware that she interrupted her mother's conversation with her brother.

"Hi, sis. How's it going?"

"It isn't," Gale said. "She's being stubborn and foolish."

"Really? One of the women journalists in our office here wants a shot at Ecklund so badly that it's embarrassing," Sky said. "She sails into orbit at the mention of the guy's name. She's a great-looking gal, too. But you don't care about that, do you, sis? When are you two leaving for Helsinki?"

"We aren't," Gale said. "Your sister is so

miserable that she's called that off."

"Hmm. Can't have it exactly the way *you* want it, eh, sis? I sure hope IISP can keep you warm during those cold, long winter nights back in New York City. Email me your flight number, and I'll meet you. Bye."

"He could learn to be subtle," Haley said, "or keep his wisdom to himself."

"You wouldn't mind," her mother replied, "if he wasn't always right."

Haley rarely shied away from decision making, and that was one reason why she so enjoyed her work at IISP. But on that day, a week after returning from Oslo, it shocked her to realize that she wanted no part of the place, and she stacked in the drawer the mail that awaited her signature. She wanted to go home, to be away from everyone. The truth was that she wanted to be with Jon, and the possibility of that seemed nil.

She remembered then that the day before she left Oslo, she raced around the city looking for a gift that she finally found and ordered for Jon. It was to have been delivered after the departure of their plane on the day that she and Gale left. Any man receiving such a gift from a woman would know that her heart was hanging on it, fragile and exposed. It had been one week already, and she didn't know whether he had received it.

"Telephone on line two, Haley."

"Take the message, Amy. I'm leaving for the day."

"But it's —"

She interrupted. "If it isn't Jon, it can wait till tomorrow." Amy lifted an eyebrow, signaling her awareness that for the past week she'd been seeing a different Haley. Haley knew she'd been acting in a way that would seem strange to anyone who knew her, but she was past caring.

"Call back, Mr. Andersen. She's on her way out."

Haley spun around. "Why didn't you say it was Nels?"

Amy knew when to be quiet, so she merely put the call on hold until Haley could retrace her steps.

"My, but we're unfriendly," Nels said when Haley answered the phone. "Isn't it too early for lunch? Where're you off to?"

"Hello, Nels. You can beat anyone I know loading questions into a single sentence. I was on my way home. I wish I had a country hideaway that I could hang out in."

"Bad as that, huh? Why don't you call Du-Pree and get the key to Jon's place in Saugerties, upstate. You can walk in the

woods, swim, whatever. And all by yourself . . . provided that's what you want. By
the way, hello, Nels. How are you? How nice
of you to call."

She had to laugh. "Sorry I was rude. It's
just that this telephone has rung incessantly
today, and I'm washed out. And another
thing, Jon has never invited me to his place
upstate."

"Did he call?"

"No."

"Now we've come to the core of the matter. I understand that he's in Bangkok, trying to whip that bureau into line. Somehow,
in my estimation at least, it doesn't meet
the standards of the other EIS bureaus. Sure
you won't join me for lunch?"

"Thanks, but no. Could I have a rain
check on lunch? I really do want to get
home."

She didn't feel like talking about Jon with
anyone. And she didn't want to discuss her
feelings or their problem. Besides, Jon had
put an end to it. He had said that he didn't
know how to crawl. That also meant that he
wouldn't respect anyone who did crawl.
Furthermore, she didn't know how to crawl,
either, and wasn't planning to learn.

"All right, love," Nels said. "But you need

to work out things with Jon. Don't put it off."

"I didn't tell you that —"

"No, you didn't tell me. But you're in love with Jon. And if you're not happy after spending a week with him and his parents in his family's home, the reason has to lie with the state of your relationship with him. I'm leaving tonight for Berlin. See you in about ten days. Chin up. And don't forget that you're a prize for any man."

She stared at the telephone before hanging up. Perhaps it was then that the truth began to penetrate her thoughts. Nels had said she was a prize. Where did men, people for that matter, put their prizes? They put them on shelves, in glass cases, in old trunks, in drawers, out of sight. Had she foolishly considered herself a prize? She ruminated about that as she made her way home. Perhaps not. But she considered IISP her prize, and she had placed it above everything. By the time she reached her apartment, she was wondering whether the price for keeping her prize might not be too high.

Several days later, Jon reached the door of his parents' home, on his way to the company limousine that was waiting in front of the house to take him to the airport. As he opened the door, he almost collided with a delivery boy who, when he'd gathered his wits, asked whether Jon Ecklund lived there. "I'm Jon Ecklund," he told him, impatiently.

"I have a package for you. It's in my van."

"Leave it with my mother. I'm in a hurry to catch a plane."

"I'm sorry, sir, but I have orders to give it only to you. And it's real perishable."

"All right, but get a move on. I don't have a minute to spare." The boy rushed back to his van and returned with a large carton that seemed to shake of its own accord. He opened the box and removed a basket, handing it to Jon.

"What the . . . ?"

"Open it, sir. He's a real beauty."

"He?" Jon lifted the basket lid and a furry little golden retriever jumped into his arms. "There must be some mistake."

"No, sir. Read the card, please."

It was then that he noticed the tag around the puppy's neck. He read, "I'm Midas. Haley wants me to look after you."

He had rarely been so deeply touched. Why had she done it? So that he'd think of her every waking moment? He would have done that anyway. So that every time he caressed that little creature with the soulful brown eyes, he'd want to touch her, love her? He didn't need prompting to want that. He looked down at the delivery boy, who was giving him a curiously questioning look. He needed a few minutes alone right now, minutes that he didn't have. He dug into his pocket, found some crowns and gave them to the smiling boy. Then he turned around and went to the kitchen where he knew he'd find his mother.

"What is it, Jon? I thought you were halfway to the airport?"

"Look at this, will you? I met the delivery boy as I was leaving." Seeing his lack of composure, she guessed the identity of the giver. Jon wasn't easily flustered.

"I'll take care of him while you're in Bangkok. What are you planning to call him?" He pointed to the tag around the puppy's neck and turned to leave. Then he stopped, reversed himself, gave his mother a light kiss of the cheek, took the puppy, gave it a hug and left.

Inger watched him go. Jon had never been fond of dogs, but she knew that he was going to love that one. "Why," she mused, "is it so difficult for them to see that they belong together?" She thought, not for the first time, that Erik's retirement had been extremely untimely.

■ ■ ■ ■

Jon glanced around at the other passengers seated in first-class — five men and one woman — and wondered absently where they were going and why. Each one sat alone, in a window seat. Each was looking out of the window, discouraging conversation with any fellow passenger. He noted that they all looked tired, bored and not a little jaded. It occurred to him that he, too, might look exactly like that in a few years — a man for whom work was everything, not because he wanted it that way, but because any other options that he might have had had long since dissolved. He accepted a glass of white wine from the ever-smiling stewardess and a napkin from the one right behind her. There were six other first-class passengers, but two of the four stewardesses seemed to think it their duty to serve him alone. Another one of life's nasty little jokes, he thought, irritably. Why did so many women go for a man's shell, his image, his visage, and not give a thought to what was going on inside of him? Both women had made it clear that they were ready to follow him off the plane. And why? They wouldn't understand his needs nor give a damn about them if they did comprehend. One of them wore at least four different shades of eye shadow. He'd bet that Haley didn't even own any. She sure as hell didn't need makeup. He hadn't seen many women who equaled her in natural beauty.

Haley. When she sent him that puppy, she might as well have sent an Australian boomerang after him. And she damned well knew it. He wondered if he'd have the strength to stay away from her. Whenever he got his hands on her, she was just like that puppy — sweet, cuddly, tender. Dear God, he couldn't let himself think about what she was like when he was loving her. That last time . . . the feeling inside of her at the apex of her passion was something that he would never forget. She was like an earthquake, erupting with violent tremors all around him, clutching and squeezing him until she drained him of his very essence. And he knew that she wouldn't forget it, either. She was out of herself, lost in him. He'd looked into her face as she came apart, every bit of reserve gone, and shook uncontrollably in his arms.

He didn't know how she could coolly stay away from him for the sake of that institute. He quickly corralled his thoughts. He did understand it, well sort of. She had a right to her profession. She had worked hard for the stature that she had attained, and he would never expect her to forsake her dreams. But she could pursue her profession and still be with him, if she'd just *give* a little. If she would only make just the smallest concession, he'd go two steps further. As soon as he walked into his Bangkok office, he telephoned her.

Haley locked her desk and had reached to turn out the light when the phone rang. He didn't wait for her to identify herself but spoke in a husky voice. "Listen, baby, I've never been one for pets, but I fell in love with that little guy as soon as I saw him. Midas, huh? I don't know what you were telling me when you sent him to me, but you really hit me where I could feel it. The little rascal jumped right into my arms. Look, sweetheart, I need you. I . . . I just need you? When you see your way clear to meet me half, no, *one third* of the way, let me know." He hung up before she could respond.

She knew that he wasn't being rude, that he was just having difficulty dealing with his emotions. She sat there for a while, lonely but happy.

■ ■ ■ ■

The next day, tired from a sleepless night and still shaken by Jon's confession that he needed her, Haley could barely get through the day. Still floating on a cloud from Jon's call, she gushed when she spoke with her mother that evening.

"Life is good, Mama. I can barely keep my feet on the ground."

"Jon or the institute?"

"Jon. I love him so much, Mama. He called me from Bangkok and . . . and he told me he loves me and needs me. I'm still . . . I thought he was still mad at me."

"Did you convince him that you loved him?"

"He didn't give me a chance. He said it and hung up."

"And I suppose you're not clever enough to dial a number in Bangkok."

"He stunned me."

"And not for the first time, either, I don't suppose. Hessy, I'd like you to consider that he needs to know he is loved just like you do. Think about that. Good night, dear."

Before Haley could reflect further, Sky called. "Mama said something unreal's going on with you and Ecklund. She told me

242

to talk to you. Is this thing really mutual? I mean, what's he telling you, sis?"

"He says he loves me and needs me and that he's waiting for me to meet him one third of the way."

"Do you love him? Really love him, I mean?"

"With every breath I take."

"Then what's wrong with your feet? You've got lead in them or something?"

"It's a long story, Sky."

"I'll just bet it is. You get your act together, sis. You love him. He needs you and you're dragging your feet. Why don't you just pin a sign on him that says 'man available'? I told you I know two women here in Washington who would take him out of circulation in a minute. And there's got to be a hell of a lot more in New York, Bangkok, Oslo and half the other major cities. Go ahead. See how long he waits. Be seeing you." He hung up.

Haley knew that her mother and her brother loved her fiercely, but she wished that they would back off about Jon. She found Sky's attitude strange, because he had never thought that any man was good enough for her. Was Jon that special, or was it because she would soon be twenty-nine? She poured a glass of wine for herself, nursed it until she became sleepy and went to bed. Sleepy, she was, but when the sun rose, she was still wide awake.

She struggled out of bed and put on a pot of coffee, but a queasiness that she'd also felt the night before took her appetite, and she settled for a glass of tomato juice. Confused and uncertain as to what course she should take, she chose the easy route and sent Jon a note. She knew that he deserved a telephone call, but she wasn't prepared to deal with her feelings for him nor his for her, because she still hadn't found a means of meeting him even one third of the way.

Out of sorts, Haley walked into her office nearly an hour before the start of the working day, wondering how she would overcome the feeling of exhaustion. As she sat down at her desk, it alarmed her to realize that the institute simply did not mean to her what it once had. She was proud of IISP, but with a sudden flash of honesty, she acknowledged that she was also resentful of it and that there had recently been times when she viewed it as an unwanted burden. Yet the thought of giving up the institute or of sharing its leadership did not occur to her. When five o'clock arrived, her relief was palpable.

■ ■ ■ ■

Haley used her key to enter her mother's house. She'd known that Gale would not be home before six o'clock but, in order to avoid the rush hour traffic, she took an early flight. She hadn't eaten any lunch, so she made a peanut butter and jelly sandwich, got a glass of milk and went in the living room to munch, watch television and relax. Over three weeks had passed, and Jon had not responded to her note.

She needed desperately to be with him. Her thoughts were of him and of what they had been to each other. "I'm happy when I'm with him," she said to herself. "Even when I'm annoyed with him, I'm happy so long as he's close by. I love to look at him, to touch him, to hear his deep voice and his lilting words. I love being with him. And oh, the way he makes me feel!"

She remembered his gentleness, the way he had cherished her and the way he had surrendered to her totally and completely. "Oh, my Lord. How did I let myself get to the point where a man meant this much to me?" The words spilled out of her in a torrent of emotion. She stood abruptly with the intention of putting the dishes in the kitchen. Gale found her on the floor fifteen minutes later. She had passed out.

Paul Blake, the Feldon family physician, removed his stethoscope, pinched his nose and informed Gale that Haley was exhausted but otherwise healthy. He prescribed a week of complete rest and three square meals a day, with no caffeine, no chocolates and no alcohol.

"I want to see her in my office nine-thirty Monday morning without fail," he added as he walked to the door.

Gale relayed the message to Haley and waited for the expected refusal and denial. It didn't come. "I have been unexplainably tired lately, Mama, but I can't be away from the institute for an entire week."

Gale took a deep breath and faced her recalcitrant daughter. "You're not leaving this town until Paul says you may. Nobody is indispensable. If you run an institute that size without delegating responsibility, you're an inefficient chief executive. I suggest you call that new employee what was her name —"

"Nina, Mom. Her name is Nina Emory," Haley said.

"Thank you. Call Nina, and tell her that you're taking a week."

Haley gave in, and it astonished Gale that she hadn't put up a fight. It was out of character, and the situation bore watching.

"You're telling me that you don't intend to tell Jon Ecklund that you're carrying his child? You're planning to have it, aren't you?" Gale asked when Haley returned from the doctor.

"How could you ask such a question? Of course I am. But I haven't heard from him since he called me three weeks ago, and I have no intention of waltzing up to him and asking him to marry me. Besides, women don't have to be married these days when they want to have a baby. Dr. Blake says that I'm in good health and shouldn't have any difficulties."

"You listen to me, Haley Feldon. You told that man you wouldn't marry him, and he still spilled his soul to you. Did you call him back and tell him that you love him? No. What do you expect? Oh, do what you want, but I don't relish being grandmother to a child who's staggering under the stigma you're laying on this one, a child who's on the defensive before it's born. Among my people, what you're contemplating is practically unknown."

Haley leaned back against her pillow,

drained. She had been in shock since the doctor told her that morning that she was pregnant. She wanted the child but would have been happier if it had come at a more convenient time. She had been too busy to wonder about the plain-as-your-face signs of pregnancy. She would have laughed if it had been funny. That last time, when she'd seduced him, she'd been so full of him, so wild in ecstasy that she fought his attempt to protect her. She wondered what price she would pay for those forbidden moments of pleasure.

Dusk had fallen when Haley awakened. After a single knock on her door, Sky walked into her room without waiting for an invitation. "What on earth are you doing here, Sky?" He stood at the head of her bed, looking down at her. He's big, she thought, just as big as Jon. And when did he get to be so handsome and so much like Papa?

"Mama said you were still here and that you weren't up to snuff. And when I asked what the trouble is, she was evasive. Mama never equivocates, so I figured something was wrong with you. What is it, sis?"

"Nothing that time won't cure," she answered, cryptically.

"Yeah? And what the hell does that

mean?" She took a deep breath, not sure how her brother would take the news. He had always been extremely protective of her, as many a broken toothed adolescent boy could verify. She loved him and needed his respect, and she realized with surprise that telling her mother was far, far easier that telling Sky. She gathered her courage and looked him in the eye.

"How do you feel about being uncle to a green-eyed, blond niece or nephew?" If she expected shock, she was disappointed.

Nothing shocked Sky Feldon. "You're pregnant?"

"About three months."

"When are you getting married?"

"I'm not. I haven't heard from him in three weeks."

Sky hunkered down beside her bed so that he could see her telltale eyes. "Now, run this by me again. He told you that he loves you and that he needs you and wanted to marry you — or so Mama said. And you interpret that to mean he's not interested?"

"If he was, he wouldn't let three whole weeks go by —"

"How much encouragement did you give him? None, I'll bet. And you conclude on the basis of nothing but your own self-indulgence that you've been rejected. Now let me tell you something, Haley. You're being damned irresponsible — irresponsible in respect to both the child and its father. You're a big girl. If you didn't want to get married, why did you let yourself get pregnant? And why the hell didn't he prevent it, anyway?"

"Now, hold it, Sky. This isn't Jon's fault. He tried his best to protect me, but I . . . I wouldn't cooperate." He observed her quizzically out of almond-shaped chocolate-brown eyes.

"When you made love with him, you trusted him to protect you. Don't you realize that he was trusting *you* to do the right thing and honor *him,* if his efforts to protect you failed? Woman, don't you know that a man hurts the same as a woman does, that he feels rejection and betrayal just as you do? How would you feel if Jon took *your* child away from *you?* What does he say about all of this, anyway?"

"I'm . . . I'm not planning to tell him. He's probably not interested in me anymore. At least that's the way he's acting."

"You're not going to tell him?" He stared at her, slowly unfolding himself from his haunches. "I see. A man of Jon Ecklund's stature deserves better. I want to be there when you watch some kid call your child a

bastard. And I want to hear you explain to your child why you thought it didn't deserve the love and caring of its father. And by the way, I care a hell of a lot more about your behaving with honor toward the man you let love you than I do about the color of your child's eyes and hair."

He didn't tell her goodbye or ask her what her plans were. He merely walked out, leaving her with the feeling that she had lost her best friend. For as long as she could remember, he had been her best friend apart from her mother. She couldn't know that by the time Sky reached his apartment he had arrived at a difficult decision.

Jon leaned against the old Norwegian spruce that had been his silent friend since before he was six years old. A well-worn black leather jacket, nondescript jeans and his favorite red-and-black plaid flannel shirt shielded him from the bitter cold and biting wind, though not entirely. He didn't mind the discomfort. His body temperature wasn't his problem. He whittled on a stick, dreading the night, as sunset neared. It was time for a decision, one that he would live with for the remainder of his life. He wanted a home, children — his own family. He loved his parents, but he couldn't remain in their home. It was their nest, not his. And he was tired of seeing the pain behind their smiles, pain for him. He pitched the stick into the stream but not before he noticed that he had been well on the way to carving the head of a woman.

Looking at the sunset, it hit him forcibly that romantic love had been considered a necessary basis for marriage only since the last century and only in most, but not all, Western cultures. Perhaps if he went about choosing a mate scientifically, he'd have more success. Using a broker, if necessary, he'd find a woman who shared his interests and have her agree in advance to accommodate his physical needs and bear his children. In exchange, he would provide her with financial security and give her his word that he would be a faithful, caring husband and father.

With heavy feet, he walked back to the house. But as he reached the back door, it occurred to him that he might not be able to keep his end of the bargain. The night after receiving Haley's note, depressed and lonely, he'd tried for the first time in his life to erase his misery in the arms of a desirable, willing woman. He hadn't wanted the woman, and none of her tricks would change that. Embarrassed, he'd simply told her the truth — he was trying to forget a love gone sour and couldn't get the woman he loved out of his thoughts.

Still in a rotten mood the next afternoon, his antenna shot up when Eva, his secretary, walked into his office rather than buzz him through the intercom as she usually did. "Jon, Sky Feldon is on the phone from Washington."

He hesitated before taking the phone. Why was Sky Feldon calling him? Blood rushed through his veins, and his heartbeat accelerated. Haley. It had to be Haley. He grabbed the phone. "What is it, Sky? Is there anything wrong with Haley?"

"She's okay, Jon, but I am calling about her." Sky paused for a moment.

"Look, man, there's no way to say this but bluntly."

Jon braced himself, unable to imagine what it could be. "All right, let's have it."

"Haley tells me that you're the father of her unborn child."

"*What! What the . . .* What the hell did you say? Never mind, I know what you said. Why are *you* calling me to tell me this? Wait a minute. Are you accusing me of —"

"Hold it, Ecklund. In my book, you're the innocent victim here, not Haley. That's why

I'm calling."

"Now, I definitely don't know what you're talking about. How is it that you know I'm going to be a father before I do? After she found out, I should have been the next person to know. Look here, she *is* going to have the baby, isn't she? *Talk to me, man!*"

Jon was no longer sitting but was pacing the floor of his office to the extent that the length of the telephone cord would allow.

"Oh, she's planning to have it, all right. The problem is that she's also planning on being an unmarried mother."

"She's planning *what?* The hell you say! When my children are born, they will have my name." He was getting angrier by the second.

"I'm with you, man. I called you because I find her position untenable. I have told her that if she goes through with this she dishonors her child and its father. I have also told her that you deserve better. She's my sister. I love her, and I would protect her at any cost, but I do not and cannot condone what she is proposing to do about this baby, and she knows it. You need to talk some sense into her — in person and soon. Mama and I did our best but to no avail. She's not even planning to tell you anything about it."

"Why? She knows that I love her, that she is the essence of my life. How can she . . . ? Oh, God! Tell me that this is just a nightmare and that I'll wake up in a minute." He paused, and then his anger surfaced again. "She won't get away with it. Damned if she will."

"I think you should know that she is telling herself that you don't care for her anymore, because she hasn't heard from you in a few weeks. Of course, she doesn't see her role in that. She also thinks that since she hasn't shown any enthusiasm for marriage when you've asked her, she can't go crawling — her words — to ask you to marry her now that she's pregnant. Assuming that you understand women better than I do, you'll sort this out. If there's anything I can do, let me know."

"I owe you one, Sky. I definitely will not forget your kindness."

"Forget it, man. We both love her and want what's right for all concerned."

"Thanks. Where is Haley right now?"

"She's with Mama in Washington." He gave Jon the address and telephone number. "The doctor says she's suffering from exhaustion and has her resting in bed for a week, but she's otherwise very healthy."

"Thank God for that. Do you know how

far along she is?"

"Three months."

"Three months? And she hasn't said a word to me about it?"

"She didn't know until yesterday."

"It's past four o'clock in the afternoon here, so I can't get a plane out of Europe today. But I'll be there tomorrow. I'd prefer that she didn't know my plans?"

"I wouldn't breathe it in my prayers. Good luck, Jon." Sky hung up.

For the next hour, Jon sat slumped in his desk chair, warring with his emotions, vacillating between anger and joy, anguish and happiness. Slowly, he accommodated himself to the fact that he was going to be a father and that he was going to have one hell of a fight on his hands.

"Come crowing hens or barking cats," he said to himself, "that baby will carry the Ecklund name."

CHAPTER 9

Haley sat up in bed hugging her knees and slowly sipping club soda in the hope that she could keep it down when her bedroom door burst open and Jon walked in.

"Where did you come from?" A shocked Haley wanted to know.

"Oslo. And don't tell me that you're happy to see me. I wouldn't believe that or anything else you tell me." He handed her some papers. "Fill in these. As soon as the doctor lets you out of bed, we'll be married. If you're not well enough to get out of bed by the end of the week, we'll get married right here in this room."

In spite of his hurt and anger, the sight of her half lying, half sitting there looking frail moved him to gather her in his arms, to love her and to protect her. But he didn't give in to the almost overwhelming need to hold her or to the temptation to forgive her for what she was trying to do to him. He stared

257

at her with blazing eyes, eyes that held no softness, eyes that were harshly accusing and judgmental.

She couldn't control the flush of her body at the sight of him, but her pride and her temper joined forces, and she lashed out. "Where do you get off storming in here and telling me what to do? Go back to wherever you were and whoever you were with for the past three weeks."

"I assume that you're referring to my non-response to that impersonal, cold and pathetic note you wrote me after I bared my soul to you. We can get married and live together beginning now or we can spar off and make a public wreck of our lives and that of our child. You decide how it will be. I will have my child."

"Even if I agreed to marry you — and I don't — I couldn't go live with you. I've got the institute to think about and the people there and elsewhere who are depending on me."

"Ah, so now we come to the real reason why you would deny me my parental rights, even the right to know that I have fathered a child. It's your precious institute, again — your own personal prized possession. You would swap your prize for your child's well-being and for the rights and happiness of the man that you swore you loved. Love! Woman, you don't know the meaning of the word."

"You have no right to speak to me this way. I can't walk away from it. It's gone further than I ever dreamed that it would."

"Right! You speak of right? You speak of dreams?" He threw back his head and laughed a hollow, mirthless laugh. "I'll tell you about dreams. To know completeness with the woman you love and who loves you. To see your babies growing in the womb of that woman, for whom you would give your life. To watch their birth and hold them the first time they cry. To walk in the woods with them, teaching them about nature and life. Dreams? Caring for your children and your woman. Loving and protecting them. Dreams? Teaching your children how to ride a horse, how to love and care for their pets. Dreams? A house in the country where it's quiet and peaceful, where your children can play without fear. Dreams? To grow old with that one wonderful woman. Tell me, Haley, how do you stack up an institute against a man's life? Since you can hold audiences spellbound with your knowledge and wisdom, let's have some of it now."

"Which one of them told you about this?"

"That's irrelevant, and you know it. Are we getting married now or not?"

"I told you —"

"Did you, now? Well, just let me tell *you.* I will not father a bastard. And I will love and care for my child before it is born as well as after its birth. You've got one week — do you hear me — one week to decide. I'll be at my place near Saugerties, in upstate New York. We get married. Otherwise, I'll let the viewers of EIS evening news international edition decide about a woman who implements programs for young, out of wedlock mothers, while she deliberately deprives her own unborn child and its father of their rights. Oh, yes, and I fully intend to name names. Then let's see what happens to that prize of yours."

She gasped. "You miserable bully! You would resort to blackmail?"

"Sure as my name is Jon Stig Ecklund. I can be as underhanded as you. And if that doesn't work, we'll go to court. I won't lose there, especially not after I testify how hard I tried to protect you and how you thwarted my efforts. Get this, Haley, and get it straight. You do the honorable thing, or I will take my baby from you. And then I will find a mother for it, one who will understand and appreciate the meaning of a father's love. I give you my word on this, and make no mistake, I keep my word."

He turned as if to leave, but having second thoughts, he reversed himself and moved to the side of her bed. With a single stroke, he threw the cover completely off her.

"How dare you? What right do you have to invade my privacy this way?"

"I have every right," he said softly, as he gazed down at her. She watched as he stood there transfixed. Slowly, he knelt beside the bed, placed his hand upon her belly and gently caressed it. Then, as if oblivious even to her presence there, he softly kissed the place where his child lay, murmuring, "I love you. Oh, I love you." Then turning his head away, as if guarding it from her, he headed for the door. Had he looked at her he would have seen her tears.

As he reached the door, he did not wonder or care how long Gale had been standing there. Her face awash with tears, she reached up and put her arms around him, guiding him to the stairs. With understanding for the weight of his sadness and the realization that he needed a friend, she led him to the kitchen and gave him a chair. Quietly, she made coffee and served them both. Finally, after the second cup, he spoke. "I can't understand this, Gale. She loves me. I know it, and she knows that I love her."

"Haley is as stubborn as a mule. When Haley takes a stand, she finds it hard to relent. But there's more here. It appears that she has lingering doubt about her attractiveness and value to a man. I think, in fact, I know that she'll come to you."

"You're not serious?"

"Yes, she will. And of her own volition. I watched her while you caressed her belly. You'll see."

"Well, I hope you're right. I don't want to hurt her in any way. I don't even know if I can go through with something that would hurt her. She's precious to me. But I meant it when I said that my child will have my name before it leaves her body."

"And you are right. When did Sky call you? We've only known this for two days."

"Ten o'clock yesterday morning, your time. I got here as fast as I could." He gave her the address and telephone number at his estate at the foot of the Catskill Mountains on the Hudson River. "I'll be there for two weeks. If she isn't there at the end of a week, I'm coming back here."

"You're not going to your New York office?"

"No. Haley is my only reason for being in the States, and she should have no doubt of that. I'm going to my place as soon as I reach Sky."

"You can call him from here." She dialed the number, gave the phone to Jon and left the kitchen. After speaking with Sky and giving him his estate address and phone number, Jon bade Gale goodbye and went to the Reagan National Airport, where a pilot waited with the company plane.

Ambling through the forest near the northwestern border of his land, Jon thought back to his childhood. Growing up with Svend had been wonderful. As small boys and best friends, they had shared everything. As close as brothers could be, he had beat up any tough boy who so much as threatened Svend and hadn't realized until he was in his late teens that Svend was a hell of a scrapper and could beat boys almost twice his size. Even now he was amused at Svend's explanation, which was that Jon enjoyed protecting him so much that he didn't want to deprive him of such pleasure.

Reflecting on the wonder of the ties that bind siblings, he became anguished. He wanted children, and he wanted them with Haley. What if she didn't come to him? Suppose she decided that she really could go on without him? What if he lost his child? To acknowledge such possibilities was like a solid blow to his solar plexus.

Leaning against an old maple, he looked around him and took a calming breath. These woods were perfect for children. They could fish in the brook that slowly meandered over the length of the estate and climb the trees. He could string up hammocks and build tree houses for them. He thought of the plans he'd had for the place before his father retired — a farm, an orchard and horses. He'd intended to make it a haven for the family he longed to have. He heard a stick crack and looked back to see a brown bear going in the opposite direction. "Well, I'm sure not up to wrestling with those guys," he said to himself, and accelerated his pace homeward.

The quiet spell just before sunrise had always been Jon's favorite time of day. He had solved many a company problem leaning against a tree and whittling on a stick as the sun began to work its magic on the early morning sky. It had always been a time that gave him strength and solace. Lately, his early morning meditation in communion with nature had also offered respite from his parents' gentle solicitude. But on this morning, he found no comfort from the beauty around him.

How would he bear the days while she made up her mind? The days? *What nonsense,* he thought. How would he endure the rest of his life? He went back into the house, got his swim trunks and raced down to his indoor pool.

After an hour of swimming and exercise, his mind was clearer. He put in a call to his mother and told her what he wanted.

"I'll have it on FedEx tomorrow morning," she promised. He got in the Volvo that he kept in his garage and drove into town.

Six days — six — and still she hadn't come. Jon began to pack his bags. As soon as he secured the house, he'd phone DuPree for the plane. He looked up at the domed ceiling of his home, and thinking that she would never see it, never share it with him, he ran his fingers through his hair in a gesture of frustration. It would be painful for both of them, but he would have his child.

"She has cast the die," he grumbled aloud. "Let the chips fall where they may. I am going to have my child one way or another." He was halfway down the stairs when the doorbell rang.

"Now what?" he asked himself, disgruntled at the prospect of being detained by a lost hiker. He yanked the door open and stared in shock. Quickly, he brought his emotions and his comportment under rigid control.

"Hi."

"Hi." They regarded each other warily and in silence until Haley breached the uneasy silence. "May I come in?"

He responded with a question of his own. "Did you pay the taxi driver?"

"Yes. It's cold out here. Aren't you going to invite me to come in?"

"If you paid him, what is he waiting for?"

"I told him to wait in case no one was home."

"Well, I'm home, so he can damn well leave now." He wanted that potential escape route closed to her. She was there now, and he intended to keep her there until they settled things, once and for all.

Apparently, his behavior disconcerted Haley. She shivered as she looked up at him, her vulnerability exposed. Recovering presence of mind, he pulled her into the house and slammed the door behind her, and in a symbolic gesture that he didn't bother to examine, he locked it.

She glimpsed his suitcase lying where he

had dropped it when he opened the door. Then she noticed that he was dressed for travel. "You were leaving? I thought you said that you would be here for two weeks."

"That's what I said. I also said that if you weren't here within a week, I would be back in Washington to get you, and that's where I was headed."

"This is just the seventh day."

"That's a week in my book, and I said within a week."

She slumped against the door, her arms folded across her breasts as if to secure warmth.

Her gesture knocked the wind out of him. "You're cold," he said, his voice laden with concern. "What was I thinking about leaving you standing out there? How did you get here? Didn't you take the company plane?"

"No. I came by train."

"But I left word with Sky about that. He was to call the company plane for you."

"My meddlesome brother doesn't know that I'm here." He almost smiled. He looked closely at her and felt a clutching at his heart as he noted her delicate skin and her frailness.

"That's an awfully long ride. You must be

exhausted. When did the doctor release you?"

"This morning, just before I left."

He could have kicked himself.

"Are you hungry? When did you last have something to eat?" He longed to take her in his arms, comfort her and love her, but he'd sworn to himself that he wouldn't touch her again until their future was settled one way or the other.

"I had something this morning before leaving, but it didn't stay down."

"It's four o'clock. You must be starving." He noticed that she shivered again. "I had turned off all of the heat, because I was leaving. Come on. I'll take you upstairs and get you warm." He placed one arm under her knees and the other around her shoulder.

"I can walk, Jon. I've got two good feet."

"I know that, but right now, you're going to use mine. It's my place to take care of you, and I'm going to do precisely that. So you make up your mind to accept it. Got that?" When she offered no further resistance, he realized how very tired she must be.

"Where are you taking me?"

"To my bedroom. I'm going to put you to bed while I get the house warm." Unable to resist, he held her a little closer as he mounted the steep stairs. Jon knew that his accelerated heartbeat didn't come from the climb to the second floor but from the knowledge that he was holding what he loved most on earth, his woman and his unborn child, in his arms. He sat her on the edge of his king-size bed, knelt and removed her boots and thick stockings. Seeing how pale her hands were, he rubbed them gently between his.

"I'll soon have it warm in here." Looking everywhere but her face in an effort to hide from her the emotions that were all but overpowering him, he carefully unbuttoned first her bulky sweater and then her silk shirt. All the while, she watched him placidly. He had not considered that she might not be wearing a bra, only that he wanted to get her comfortable as quickly as possible. When her breasts fell into his hands, he had to stifle his sudden desire. Lust wasn't what she needed. Trying not to remember how he felt while he kissed and sucked them, he betrayed himself, staring like a teenager.

"They, they're . . . I mean, aren't they bigger? They look like they're going to pop. Is it because of the baby?" he asked softly in awe, finally looking directly into her face.

"Yes. The doctor said they're supposed to

get larger."

"Has the baby grown any?" he asked, barely above a whisper. "I mean, are you getting bigger already? Do you think I could . . . ?" His voice drifted off in uncertainty.

Her eyes caressed the face that was so dear to her and she saw his eager joy and the brilliant sparkles that threatened to drop from his eyes to his cheeks. "How could I have even considered depriving him of this experience?" she asked herself. Slowly, so as not to disturb her balance, she stood. He looked at her inquiringly, standing as she had done. He was unprepared for her action as she took his right hand and carefully laid it upon her belly.

"Haley, oh Haley." He gently stroked the firm little mound, marveling at the change in just one week. "It's hard. Is it supposed to be hard like this? Shouldn't we get a specialist to see if everything's all right?"

She laughed a gay, happy, carefree laugh. "That's protection for the fetus. I'm fine."

He threw the covers back, picked her up and laid her in bed. Then he got one of his pajama tops, and after removing her blouse, he put it on her. He knelt beside the bed.

"Thank you for sharing this with me."

He covered her carefully and then placed a goose down comforter over her.

"What can you eat?" he asked, his eyes loving her face.

"Toast, soda crackers, stuff like that. Maybe I could drink some club soda. I like mint tea, but I can't have caffeine. Oh! Jon, if you're going out, could I please have some peach ice cream and some anchovies?"

He grimaced. "*Anchovies?* You planning on making pizza?" Then understanding slowly dawned upon him, and he laughed. "Good grief, honey, don't tell me that my kid's got a yearning for anchovies? My mother said that I drove her crazy with my craving for anchovies when she was carrying me. Can you believe this?"

Jon was grinning and beaming with pride. He patted her gently on the shoulder and set about lighting a fire in the fireplace.

"You'll soon be warm. Will you be all right if I leave you for a little while? The grocer is just about ten minutes away, and I want to get some food into you. The only food in the house is in the freezer. I'm going to lock the front door behind me. If for any reason you have to get out of the house, use the kitchen door. Got it?"

She nodded. "Where's the bathroom?"

271

it's that door beside the closet."

"Open it for me, please. When I have to go, I'm usually in a big hurry." He walked back to the bed, concern evident on his face. "Does it happen often?"

"It's only temporary. Not to worry." She smiled, and his heart kicked over. She wanted his child. A herd of buffalo won't get her away from me, he thought, belligerently. She's mine. Unable to resist touching her, he tweaked her nose and went out, whistling as he did so.

Haley heard the hum of the motor as Jon pulled away from the house. She sat up, marveling at the turn of events. She had to rethink everything now. Her idea of a compromise wasn't going to work. It was clear that Jon not only wanted to take care of her but that he needed to do it. And he needed to be a part of her journey to motherhood. She didn't see how she could spoil his joy with suggestions for a part-time marriage. She hadn't been prepared for the extent of Jon's protectiveness or for her reaction to it. She had reveled in it. What else didn't she know about herself? When he'd removed her boots and clothing, put his pajamas on her and tucked her in bed, she had felt like a queen, sensing how he loved and cherished her. She'd felt sheltered and cared for, wrapped up in his sweetness and love. And she knew in her heart that it wasn't only because of the baby. Each time he'd made love with her, he had shown gentleness, a tender caring that had bound her to him. And she knew that he could be tough when he wanted to be, because she saw the granite side of him when she abused his feelings for her.

She pulled the comforter up to her neck, even though she knew that the chill she felt came not from the room temperature but from finally realizing the magnitude of the error she had almost made. She had to come up with another solution, and she didn't have hours in which to do it. Exhausted, she soon fell asleep.

Jon stood looking down at her as she slept, the bags of groceries still in his arms. He hadn't even stopped in the kitchen. "There's no going back," he said softly, partly to himself and partly to her. She turned to her side, hugging the pillow. The tenderness that he felt for her clutched at him, and he quickly left the room. If he didn't get out of there, he knew he'd be in that bed with her in seconds. He returned soon with a thermos of mint tea and some soda crackers.

Moving quietly so as not to disturb her, he removed his sneakers, shirt and jeans and was down to his briefs when Haley opened her eyes. She regarded him sleepily. Suddenly, she raised herself up and supported herself on one elbow as if the better to gaze at him while he finished undressing.

"Like what you see?"

Caught out, she opted for bravado. "Ab-so-lutely! But I'd like it better if there were more of you showing. How about finishing that strip tease?"

He laughed. "Behave yourself, woman. You're interfering with my self-control." He walked over to the bed and poured some of the mint tea for her. "Try this, and let's see if it works."

He sat on the edge of the bed and still wearing only his briefs, he looked down at her, his gaze cool and distant.

"Haley, I don't think I can wait any longer to know what you've decided. I'm asking you one last time to be my wife, to live with me and have my children. You will have my love, fidelity and devotion for as long as I live."

"I realize that what I had in mind when I came here will not be acceptable to you. It isn't even acceptable to me now. I don't want us to be separated any more than you do. Will you help me to find a solution for the institute? It has always meant so much to me, you know that. But in recent weeks, I have almost resented it as a barrier between us. I . . . oh, Jon, I've been so lonely for you. I missed you so. And I've been so ashamed of myself for taking advantage of you that . . . that last time we were together. My only excuse was that I wanted you so badly. Still, I know that it wasn't a fair thing to do unless I was prepared for marriage."

"And you're prepared for it now?"

He held his breath. One word and he would know his future.

"If you can tell me that you forgive my selfishness, my foolishness in not telling you, not planning to tell you about the baby. . . . I don't know what I was thinking about. When I saw how you wanted to love it, care for it and for me, I was sick with remorse. You'll be a wonderful father. And I'll be proud to be your wife, bear your children and share your life."

He sat deathly still, hardly blinking an eye. He didn't want any misunderstanding. He was too close to realizing his dream to have it vanish because of an oversight.

"Are you making our finding a solution for the institute a condition for marrying me?" he asked, unable to control the nervous tremor in his voice.

"There are no conditions. I love you and want to be with you forever."

He pulled her out of the bed and into his arms. Unable to speak, he hugged her wordlessly. Her left hand found his nape, while she wove her fingers into his thick hair.

"Haley, if you only knew how I feel!" His lips gently kissed her eyelids, cheeks, the tips of her ears and then her throat. Unable to remain still, she moved closer to him, but he stepped away from her.

"Baby, don't. You know we can't go all the way, and I'm so hungry for you."

He tried to break from her altogether, but she refused to release him. Instead, she climbed up his body and wrapped her legs around his waist, fitting the apex of her thighs to his groin.

"Hold it, baby! I'm human, and I'm starving for you. We can't think of ourselves. We've got to think of the baby."

"What does the baby have to do with this?"

"I could hurt you and cause you to lose it."

"No, you won't. The doctor told me that we didn't have to take special care until the sixth month."

He put more space between them.

"The doctor didn't know that we have a special problem. And when did he say that, anyway?"

"This morning. And I told him everything."

He looked at her with a smile slowly lighting his face. She had come to him fully prepared for every eventuality. She wiggled against him, and he knew from his last encounter with her that she intended to get what she wanted.

She slid down his body, eased away from him slightly and began to stroke him. Already fully aroused, she could feel him pulsating, almost ready to explode. What a man, she thought, for even as he fought for control, he laid her gently on the bed and knelt above her.

"Stop me if I'm doing anything wrong."

"Like what? What could you do that's wrong?"

She reached up and pulled his mouth down to hers, parted his lips with her tongue and took possession of his passion. He tried to hold back, but she was having none of that. She took his penis into her hands, caressed and stroked him until he moaned.

"Stop or I'll spill it. Give me a chance to fire you up."

He kissed his way down her body until he reached his goal, and she held her breath, waiting for the moment when he would thrust his tongue into her. Then he plunged into her, rhythmically, bringing her to the edge but denying her the release she needed.

"Stop torturing me," she begged. "I'll die if you don't let me have it."

He kissed his way up her body, stroking and teasing until she grabbed his penis and forced it into her body. When he would have slackened the pace of entry, she wrapped her legs around him and shattered his resistance. He began a gentle thrust, but she moved urgently beneath him. The pulsating rhythm of her approaching ecstasy and the clawing that always drove him wild began at once, and her cry filled the room. She moaned. Heat flushed the bottoms of her feet, her thighs began to shake and a sinking, dying feeling pervaded her. She tried to make herself come.

"Relax, Haley, and let it come. Give yourself to me." The swelling began and then the pumping and squeezing and then the ecstasy.

He had no choice but to give in to it and to the vortex of physical and emotional upheaval that was bringing him to the brink. In a strangled voice, he half pleaded, half sobbed her name. "Honey, are you with me? I can't stand this," he moaned.

As the powerful tremors shook her, she gave herself to him, exploding in his arms. "Jon, Jon, I love you, I love you!"

Succumbing to the awesome force of his rapture, he cried out. "Haley, my wife, my own, my love," he said and, in a state of near oblivion, gave her the essence of himself.

He lay on his back holding her to his side. Their time had finally come. He said a silent prayer of thanks. How could he have known in those days when he saw her and desired her from a distance that she would come to mean everything to him? He leaned over, reached into the drawer of his night table and took out a small red velvet box. He opened it and looked at the two carat diamond solitaire engagement ring that his grandfather had given to his maternal grandmother. After receiving it from his mother, he'd had it and the matching diamond wedding band altered to Haley's larger size. He rose, took her hand and knelt by the bed. And as he looked into her beloved, smiling eyes, he placed the diamond on her finger. "I love you, Haley Feldon. From now on, you belong to me and I belong to you."

ABOUT THE AUTHOR

Gwynne Forster is a national bestselling author of forty-four works of fiction — thirty-four romance novels and nine mainstream novels, including her latest, *When the Sun Goes Down.* She has won numerous awards for fiction writing, including a Gold Pen Award and an *RT Book Reviews* Lifetime Achievement Award, and has been inducted into *Affaire de Coeur* magazine's hall of fame. A demographer by profession, she is formerly a senior United Nations officer, where she was chief officer in charge of research in Fertility and Family Planning studies. Gwynne is author of twenty-seven publications in demography. She holds bachelor's and master's degrees in sociology and a master's degree in economics/demography. As an officer, first for United Nations and later for the International Planned Parenthood Federation of London, England, Gwynne traveled and/or worked in sixty-three countries. She lives in New York with her husband, who is her true soul mate.